PRAISE FOR

All the Rivers Flow into the Sea

"Lush with natural detail and alive with crisp dialogue, in an unforgettable journey where cultures clash in affairs of the heart."

—**JOHN BALABAN**, recipient of The Academy of American Poets' Lamont Prize and William Carlos Williams Award

"*All the Rivers Flow into the Sea* is an extraordinary collection. The stories are fully rendered and finely nuanced, populated with vibrant characters shaped by war or haunted by tragedy. Their voices are as vivid as the landscapes the author conjured, at once exotic yet intimately familiar, all bound by threads of love and compassion. This is one of those rare collections I would keep and read again.

—**ANDREW X. PHAM**, winner of Kiriyama Pacific Rim Book Prize and finalist for the The National Book Critics Circle Awards

All the Rivers Flow into the Sea & Other Stories

Khanh Ha

All the Rivers Flow into the Sea

Khanh Ha

©2022
All Rights Reserved.

FICTION

ISBN 978-1-958094-02-0

BOOK DESIGN & COVER: EK LARKEN
AUTHOR PHOTO: PHUONG THUY NGUYEN
COVER IMAGE: SHUTTERSTOCK

EastOver Press encourages the use of our publications in educational settings.
For questions about educational discounts, contact us online:
www.EastOverPress.com or info@EastOverPress.com.

PUBLISHED BY

EASTOVER
— PRESS —

Rochester, Massachusetts
www.EastOverPress.com

For Dan Pope

The Stories

Grateful acknowledgment is made to
the following publications, in which
the stories of this collection
originally appeared:

"The Woman-Child" (*Orison Books Anthology*)
"All the Pretty Little Horses" (*Long Story*)
"The Dream Catcher" (*ARDOR*)
"The Devil's Mask" (*Squawk Back*)
"The Girl on the Bridge" (*Mobius*)
"Night, This River" (*Bayou Magazine*)
"The *Yin-Yang* Market" (*Lunch Ticket*)
"A Mute Girl's Yarn" (*Blue Mesa Review*)
"A Scent of Long-Ago Love" (*FRiGG Magazine*)
"The Children of Icarus" (*Mount Hope*)
"All the Rivers Flow into the Sea" (*Thrice Fiction*)

The Woman-Child

1

*C*hú oi!"
    Over me, a haloed figure stood silhouetted against the sun's glare. A girl's face slowly came into focus. I pushed myself up, my back warmed by the stone well in the rising morning heat.

"Why're you sleeping out here?" The helping girl looked down at me.

"A centipede crawled on my face last night."

The girl sat down on her haunches. The briny air fanned my face.

"So, I turned on the light," I said. "No electricity. Used my Zippo, and guess what I saw on the floor? Cockroaches. Bigger than my big toe."

"So? Every house has them, *chú.*"

She called me *uncle.* I was only twenty-three. I couldn't tell her age, though, for she had a thin body of a child and a woman's face. Her long-lashed eyes brooded. At the inn she ran errands, cleaned the lodge. She wore her usual red kerchief around her head. "Daddy made me wear it so sand won't get in my hair," she once said to me. "So I don't have to wash it every day." She wore her hair past her shoulders, sometimes in two plaits.

"I forgot to ask. What's your name?" I said. I met her a week before.

She said nothing.

"Everyone has a name," I said, bringing my knees to my chest and plugging a cigarette between my lips. She watched me click open my Zippo, her gaze following my hand. I blew the smoke upward. "You remember my name?"

"Yes, *chú*."

"Say it."

"Minh."

I blew a series of small rings toward her.

"That's pretty," she said, lifting her face to see where the rings went.

"You forgot your name? You not yourself today?"

"That's not funny."

I tapped the ash and saw it drift and cling to her peach-yellow blouse in gray specks.

"I'm sorry," I said. "Let me."

She shrank back. "Daddy smokes too," she said, flicking her gaze at me. "But he never takes the cigarettes out of his mouth. He has ashes all over his shirts. They burn holes in them."

I flicked open the Zippo, then clicked it shut. "What does he do for a living?"

"He's a fisherman."

She held herself still, hands clutching the hem of her blouse to hold the scattered ashes. She looked up at me and grinned mischievously.

I shook my head. "What do I call you?"

"Does it matter?" she said.

"I don't even know how old you are."

"Do you have to know?"

"Sure, if you want to be my friend."

"I have friends. And we don't care how old we are. We never ask."

I rolled my eyes and took a last drag. I looked at the burn on her left cheek. "How'd you get burned there?" I asked, pointing to my cheek.

She shook her head.

"It's a different culture here, eh," I said.

"What're you saying? Aren't you Vietnamese too, *chú?*"

"Yeah, I am. But I left Vietnam when I was seven."

"How come you speak Vietnamese so well?"

"Because my parents are Vietnamese," I said, grinning, and it seemed to irk her.

"Are you really from America?"

Now, I stared at her as I lit another cigarette.

"Prove it," she said.

I was about to tell her to forget it, but then, with a sigh, I dug my driver's license out of my wallet. "Here."

She leaned forward, her eyebrows knitted in appraisal.

"Can you read English?" I asked.

Her lips formed silent words. She flipped the plastic sleeve, stopped at the next one. Her head canted to one side. "Who is she?"

"My girlfriend."

"She's pretty. Her hair's not yellow, though."

"She's a brunette."

"What's her name?" She perked up.

"Do you have to know?"

She pushed away my hand. "You're mean," she said sharply. "I hate you."

On the table that sat under the eaves of the inn's rear veranda was a brass pail. It was half-full of well water. A tin can floated in it. I dipped the water with the can, rinsed my mouth, gargling, and brushed my teeth. With the water left in the pail, I washed my hair.

"You don't have long hair like me," she said. "Why waste water?"

"I got sand in my hair," I said, combing its wet strands back with my fingers. "I was down on the beach last night. So windy. You should wash your hair every day, too."

"Easy for you to say, *chú*. Clean water is treasured here."

"Where'd you get your water?"

"From a public well." She glanced toward the lodging house's well. "It has a pump like that one, and it's always crowded there. I go there very early in the morning, but not this morning."

As I wiped my face with my hand, I could see her frown. Then she stamped her foot.

"What's wrong?" I said.

"You didn't ask me why I didn't go to the well this morning."

"Why didn't you go?"

She pointed at the empty pail. "Where'd you get the water from?"

"From that well. The landlord, she always leaves a pailful on the table. Every morning."

"You want another pail, *chú*?"

"Um, yes. I'm thinking of washing myself again. It's getting hot."

"Try the pump. See if you can get any water."

"I got it. That pump needs electricity to work." I laughed, remembering the outage last night.

At first, she just looked at me, sullen. Then she laughed a small, clear laugh.

"Guess I can't wash myself until we get the electricity back, eh?" I said. "Such a shame they don't have a winch for the well. If you can't use the electric pump during the outage, you can haul water by hand with a crank. Next time bring a bucket, and I'll get you water from the well here to take home. No wait."

"Why're you so kind, *chú*?"

"Haven't you been around nice people?"

"You guessed wrong, *chú*. People here are nice. Daddy is nice, very nice."

"And Mom?"

She gave me a dark look. "Just Daddy," she said finally.

"What about Mom?"

She looked disturbed. Her eyelashes batted. She unknotted her kerchief and knotted it again. It fluttered in the breeze coming in steadily now from the sea.

"Where is she?" I said.

"Daddy said never talk about her. Said he doesn't know

her."

The way she rushed the words kept me from asking any more questions. I glanced at the empty pail, then up at her. "Guess I'll be heading into town later on. At least they have electricity there."

"It'll be back on before evening, *chú*. Around here, nobody likes even days."

"Now I know. I'd better stock up water and wash myself on odd days, then."

"I must get going," she said, opening the safety pin on her blouse's front pocket. She took out a wad of money in rolled-up bills and counted them. Nodding, she stuffed them back into her pocket and fastened it with the pin. "I'm going to the market. You want anything there, *chú*?"

"Why are you so kind?"

"*Chú!*" She stomped her foot.

"Can you get me two packs of cigarettes?" I took out my wallet. "I wonder if . . . ."

"They have the kind of cigarettes you smoke, *chú*."

"How d'you know what kind I smoke?"

"I saw the pack."

I placed the money in her hand. "Do you cook?"

She didn't answer as she carefully added my bills to her bundle of cash. Her long, tapered fingers had dirt under the nails, some bitten down. But cooking? She had a stick-thin body. A child, or rather a teenager, or perhaps a woman al-ready. She was fastening the safety pin, smoothing the front of her blouse. I couldn't help noticing the tiny breasts. She lifted her eyes and fixed me with a stare.

"I cook, *chú*. Are you surprised? I cook for Daddy."

"You have time?"

"I make time stand still."

"Really?"

"When Daddy comes home from the sea, he's too tired. He's out to sea before sunrise, back at sunset. Well, you know how long each day is for a fisherman, *chú*?"

"I'm beginning to know."

"I help the woman owner here during the day. I take care of Daddy in the evening."

"Where is Mom?" I asked again.

"She's not with us."

The girl crossed the back court, passed the well, and slipped down the dirt path overgrown with cogon grass so tall it hid her from view, then she reappeared, walking on the sand where patches of spider flowers bloomed yellow. Her figure grew smaller as she crossed the pumpkin patch, the pumpkins bright orange against the glare of white sand.

2

I stood in the narrow doorway of their small hut, watching the helping girl clean her daddy's infected toe. He had passed out. "Drunk," she said. Every evening.

Twilight. The briny air was warm. Voices of the sea in the distance—the sound of crashing waves, the winds hissing through the dune grass, a sudden cry of a shore bird.

She picked up a canvas bag and slung it over her shoulder. "I must fix Daddy's net."

Outside, dusk was falling. Her red kerchief looked darker.

"Which way to the wharf?" I asked.

"This way's shorter, *chú*."

"I never noticed the shrimp ponds around here."

"I don't like seeing them."

"Why?"

"I hate them."

"Because they pollute the water?"

Her lips crimped, and she shook her head.

"Don't you care?" I asked. "Those pesticides and chemical wastes from shrimp farms?"

"No." She glanced at me. "I live here, *chú*, I know."

"But you don't care?"

"Why d'you care, *chú*?"

I never told her the purpose of my visit of Vietnam. That I was to write my thesis on Vietnam's environmental degradation caused by shrimp aquaculture. Twenty years after the war. Half a million hectares of coastal mangrove forests had been razed to become prawn farms to feed the American market.

She must have known also that beyond the seaside, toward inland, shrimp farms had encroached the mangrove forests where fish and other marine life live and spawn, the forests for centuries protecting the inland from tidal waves, from wicked storms.

"Daddy said there're so many dead fish in the ocean now. Chemical wastes from those shrimp farms kill them." She paused "Daddy will kill those shrimpers. He will." Her face looked serious.

Moral advice percolated in my head, but not a word left my mouth. I knew nothing about their lives here. Going down the foredune, I could smell a tang of fish odor, a damp smell of kelp in the air. Fishing nets were piled up above the high-tide mark, and beneath them lay ocean litter: seaweed, soggy sticks, bits of crabs' claws. High tide was coming in, tinkling through the orphaned seashells studding the sand. I stopped when something scurried out from under the mass of wet nets. A rat. The girl followed its trail and said the rat was out looking for birds' eggs, those that nested above the high-tide line. A buoy clanged, its desolate sound guiding fishermen ashore.

Her father's boat rested on the sand among others, its bow leaning down on a pair of wooden stakes. A net draped its length, spreading over the sand. Above the water, the wharf shone bluish under the iron lanterns, and in their pale illuminations she inspected the net, her brow creased, hooking her fingers in the twines of rips.

"Fresh tears?" I asked her.

She scratched her head, then said, "I haven't had time to fix them," as she swung her bag down and dropped it on the sand.

"Anything I can do for you?"

"I can do this faster on my own. You'll get in my way if you help, *chú*."

I asked if it took long. She looked at me, tilting back her head. "I wish you could fix a net just once and see how that'd do to your back after hours sitting on your knees."

"And how much did you get paid?"

She shook her head sadly, said, "*Chú*, different sizes, different fees," and then, pointing at the worn-looking net, said, "That net is about the length of five arm stretches. I got fifteen thousand *đồng* to fix the rips and recrimp the leads."

"A dollar," I said.

"It isn't much where you come from, *chú*."

I said nothing, just looking at her headscarf, now a bruised red; the light blue of her short-sleeved blouse that hugged her scrawny body; the copper-tan of her skin; the long fingers that held the scissors as she snipped off the loose tag ends, cutting them off here and there all the way to the knots of each mesh. She did this quickly, cleanly.

I asked if she'd throw away the net damaged by a sizable hole. She put away the mending needle as if she didn't hear me, and then slowly she began removing the guiding twine that had been threaded through the meshes. Finally, she spoke without looking up. "You never throw away a net, *chú*. It's like throwing away our money."

"Okay, then," I said. Annoyed by her testy mood, I decided not to ask what she or her father would do with such a damaged net.

"Don't you want to know how I'd fix a large hole, *chú*?" She turned to me, her arms akimbo.

"Yes, I do."

"I'll patch it. It takes much longer to patch it."

"Why?"

"It's hard for me to explain. You must see it, *chú*. Like you first trim the hole into a square. Then, you cut out a patch from a scrap net; its edges must match the edges of the hole so when you lay the patch in, it fits. Then, you can weave."

"How often did you have to do that?"

"Few times. Took a whole evening."

"Out here by yourself?"

"Yes, *chú.*"

I nodded. My words sank back. Not pity, but helplessness. Had she, this woman-child, ever gone to school? Had she the time to rest? What did she dream when she slept?

"Would you like to go to school?"

"Yes, *chú.*" Her quiet tone surprised me. "I hope someday I would be able to." She started looping the guiding twine around the mending needle and then tossed them into the bag. She spoke into the bag. "The innkeeper wanted to raise me and put me through school. But Daddy wouldn't allow that."

"I see. Well, he can't do much without you . . . ." *Useless ass!* I stopped before those words left my lips.

"She loves me like her own daughter."

"But she doesn't have a daughter."

"No, *chú.* How could she? She never married!"

I chuckled at her clarity. "Do you love her like you love your mom?"

Her eyes suddenly narrowed like a cat's eyes. "I don't love her," she said.

"Who?"

"Mom."

"And why's that?"

She picked up her bag and slung it over her shoulder.

We walked back up the dune, stepping over clumps of brown seaweed, our feet kicking up sand, sending sand fleas flitting across the sand. Then, her voice came. "Mom ran off. She lives with a shrimper now."

3

Twilight. On the lee side of the foredunes sheltered by tall hedgerows of vetiver grass, the sandpipers rested. An early mist hung pale over the wharf. The waves broke in empty booms against the wharf's pilings and the buoys clanged.

She wasn't alone by her daddy's boat. A man came at her, and she backed away, jabbing the mending needle at him.

I ran across the sand. She turned around to pull on the net, and he lunged for her from behind and pulled down her pants. I stumbled and regained my footing and saw her swing around, her arm flying across the man's face. She saw me and quickly pulled up her pants.

He was an old man. Dropping down on the sand, he cupped the side of his face with his hand. I stood over him. A small, gaunt-looking man. His sweat-stained brown shirt had holes on the front like cigarette burns. The wind blew sand in my face. His unwashed body smelled of alcohol.

"You leave her alone," I said to him. "Or I'll break every bone in your body."

"Yeah? Ain't done nothin' to her, ain't I?" he slurred in his twang. "And look at what she done to me. Look." He moved his hand off the side of his face. There was a dark red gash from the tip of her mending needle.

I picked up her lantern and brought it close to his face. "You're lucky," I said. "You could've been blind in one eye. Now get lost."

He scrabbled around as if he had lost something. Then, his hand came up with a squat-looking bottle. He shook it, then twisted open the cork and sniffed, muttering into the empty bottle as he staggered away. I watched him lick the bottle's neck as he bobbed across the sand, then disappeared between the dark hulks of docked boats.

The girl looked calm as she adjusted her headscarf. "How'd you know I'm out here, *chú?*"

"I didn't see you at the lodging house. The owner said you didn't come today."

"I was there today. Cooked and washed dishes."

"She said you weren't there. Said you'd probably be out in the pumpkin patch. Were you?"

"I was yesterday. But not today."

She got paid to help load up the trucks with pumpkins just harvested. I had seen them. Those ripe pumpkins weren't light, their deep orange rinds hard and hollow sounding when thumped. She said she worked the whole day until her back gave. Then, she said, "The inn owner has moments like that. She's got today mixed up with yesterday."

I brushed the sand off my face.

"Don't you have a handkerchief, *chú?*" she said. "It's very windy tonight."

"I'll bring one next time. Who's that guy? A hobo?"

"You can say that, *chú*. He's drunk most of the time." She knotted a corner of a mesh with a twine and snipped it with her scissors. "One time when I was younger, eleven, twelve, he almost got me good. That evening I was coming down the dune over there to look for Daddy, and he jumped out on me from behind a filao tree. Drunk as a skunk. That good-for-nothing old buzzard."

"Then?" I squinted my eyes at her.

"He got my legs locked with his so I couldn't crawl away, and, and . . . ."

"Pulled your pants down?"

"Yes, *chú*. I threw sand in his face. There was something hard in the sand, a horseshoe crab shell. And then as he bent to try to, to . . . I hit his face with the crab shell, and he fell off me."

"Did you tell your daddy?"

"Daddy knew he was crazy ever since Daddy was a boy. Said next time just outrun him. That old drunkard."

I shook my head, told her that if it'd happened in America, he'd have been locked up for good. She said, "Because America is rich." Then asked, "Did you see anything, *chú?*"

"See what thing?"

"What he did to me."

"Yes."

"Chú! You saw?"

"Well, you asked me."

"No, you didn't see. Okay?"

"Okay. I didn't."

"Can you help me hold the net down?"

"Certainly."

There was a large rip toward the center of the net, still

damp, heavy from seawater and smelling of fish. She'd cut out a patch from some throwaway net, and the patch was draped over the gunwale. As she put the patch in place, I said, "Such a big hole. What happened?"

"It was rough out there today," she said. "Daddy didn't go out far. He set the net closer to shore. Lots of sharp rocks near the shore."

I watched her weave. There was a dry sound of wings beating overhead, and looking up I saw a lone gull flying out into the darkening ocean. Straggling fishing boats were coming home, bobbing past the buoys toward the wharf, where several gulls were already perched on the pilings, waiting. In a moment, they would shriek with pleasure when the fishermen hauled up their seines heavy with fish.

It was dark when she finished mending the net. The waves swelled, and the wind blew out her lantern. She lit it again, her face suddenly awash in the orange illumination, her eyes a wet brown. I asked her if she had had dinner. She said yes, nodding. Then, she opened her canvas bag, rummaging around with her hand, and came up with two packs of cigarettes.

"They finally had them today at the market," she said. "The kind you smoke, *chú*."

I took the packs from her bony hand and said, "Thank you." I tried to put money in her bag, but she refused to take it. As she pushed my hand away, I said, "I still don't know your name."

"Didn't you ask inn owner?"

"Why can't I ask you?"

"You'll laugh."

"Well. I promise I won't."

She slung the bag over her shoulder and briskly footed across the sand. We moved toward the boat rows, the wind-blown sand gritty on my face, and I stopped until she turned around.

"Look," I said, speaking louder over the wind, "if you don't tell me your name, I'll make up a name for you."

She stood in one place like a statue, lantern in hand, the

sand aglow at her feet. As she turned to head up the beach, she said, "Cam."

Cam. Orange. "Why d'you think I'd laugh?" I asked her. "It's a weird name."

I thought so myself but said nothing. She looked down at her feet, then bent, hovering the lantern over the sand. A ghost crab, sand-colored, was coming out of a burrow, its eyestalks trembling like two black peppercorns as it froze momentarily in the lantern light. You couldn't tell it from the sand until it sprinted down the slope.

"Where's he going?" I asked her.

"Follow him, *chú*," she said, smiling for the first time.

I couldn't see the ghost crab very well, as if it had blended with the sand. But she paced after it in a straight line, the lantern raised high, and soon we stepped onto the damp sand now as dark as the color of water. Three feet away was the pale crab barely above the tide line where waves washed in, died, and trailed back. Suddenly, the crab sped backward, farther and farther up the sand flat, turned a sharp angle, and stopped in front of a drenched heap of perforated, round-leafed sea lettuce.

"Don't come near him," she said, looking back at me. "He can see you."

"Can he?" I looked again at its round eyestalks. I turned to her and laughed. "I think he is going for a bath."

"Daddy said he needs water to breathe. I mean, the, the . . . ."

"Air, oxygen?"

"Yes. In the water."

I took a step up, and she grabbed my arm. "Don't scare him, *chú*. Let him get his meal."

"Eating sea lettuce?"

"No. He eats beach fleas, mole crabs. They hide in those seaweeds."

"I'm going back to the inn."

"I'm going with you."

As we cut across the sand, the crosswind blew out her

lantern. She fumbled for the matchbox. In the blackness, the sea glowed in a long swath of light, pulsing like stars. I called out to her. Beyond the wharf, veiled in a white mist, the ocean was burning with an electric light of ghostly cold blue and glittering red and frosty green. She said those were sea lamps. The luminescent planktons, she added. I said I wished I could capture the magical sea lamps with a camera.

"You ever seen sea lamps back in America?"

"No. I'm sure they're there. At the right time. I wish I were there."

"With her?"

"My girlfriend?"

"Yes."

"Would be lovely."

"When are you going back, *chú?*"

I thought, then shrugged. "I don't have a date. Soon though."

"Are you going to marry her soon?"

I glanced at her. "Why are you interested?"

"I hope you'll marry her. If you don't, you'll break her heart."

"What if she doesn't want to marry me?"

"You're a man, *chú.* You can take it."

"Like your dad?"

"Yes. Except he gets drunk to forget her."

"So, men aren't tougher than women."

"They are, but women have more to lose."

I grinned in the dark as I walked by her side.

We walked in silence. After a while she said, "What's her name?"

"Her name? April."

She said the name to herself. "Do American names have meaning?"

"Some do. Her name does. *Tháng tu*, the month. And it means spring for new life."

"What's she doing in America?"

"She studies, a senior in college." Then, smiling, I shook

my head. "She's a student."

"I know she's a student. And what d'you do, *chú*?"

"I'm working on my master's degree. Well, forget that. I'm a student too."

"So, you have to go back to school after summer."

"Yes."

She was quiet as we left the dunes. I could smell a strong, musky smell; when I asked her what it was, she said nothing. We walked past the pond's shimmering liquid edge, which wrinkled when fish and frogs plopped into it. In the lull, I heard peepers and crickets and bullfrogs in the undergrowth.

The musky smell came back. I sniffled. She said that was a fox's smell and that he must be somewhere on the dune. She said sometimes if he is near and if you keep still, you could hear the soft padding of his feet on the filao needles. She knew it was a particular cross fox, his fur smoke-colored, slate-gray down his back and across his shoulders. Sometimes in the evening, when she was out on the beach, fixing the net, she'd see him hunting for fish washed up on the shore or beach rats, which he loved. He ruled the dunes at night. In the early morning, you could see his tracks in the sand, and, if you followed them, you could tell his habitual itinerary. I asked her how she could tell his tracks from the tracks made by other carnivorous animals. She said, "I'll tell you next time. Just come out at first light."

I couldn't help thinking of her independent life and the fox. We made it around the marsh, dense now with a heavy fog. Blurred figures on stilts stirred among the grasses that fringed the pond. The lamplight had spooked the night herons, and I could smell their stench on the wind as we walked into the dense fog.

There was no light behind the window shutters of the lodging house. We went up on the veranda and stood listening. "Everyone must be in bed now," I said. We stood apart, like two strangers.

By the pond behind the dune, people came to wash clothes. When it didn't rain for days on end, they fetched water from the pond for cooking and drinking. The helping girl washed her clothes there. I knew clean water was at a premium and told her politely not to use the pond water except to wash clothes. She said she knew that stagnant water gave people pink eye and diarrhea.

At the pond, without soap, she had to wash her soiled laundry twice. She kept checking her rolled-up pants for wetness, carefully wiping her hands with a washcloth, only to soak them again as she scrubbed woolen blankets until her fingertips wrinkled. I'd noticed that a hanging thread on a blouse, a loose shirt button, made her fret.

"Are you afraid to get wet?" I asked.

She looked at me and back at her hands. "*Chú*," she said, "you do this when you don't have washers like in America."

She went to the other side of the pond where the water was still and filled the pail with water there. She carried the pail back, plodding along in her new wooden clogs while other women at the pond walked barefoot. I looked at their cracked heels, at the black lines filled with dirt. I guessed she did not want any of that—her fastidious nature.

"I'll go look for bull nuts, *chú*."

"What for?"

She puckered her pretty lips, thought for a moment, then turned and walked to one end of the pond where water caltrop grew in abundance. Glossy and black, their shells curved like a leering goat-horned devil. Folks made necklaces from the already dried, oiled nuts and sold them to tourists.

With a basket of washed clothes under her arm, she walked to the fringe of the pond and carefully left her sabots and the basket on the rim before wading with her pant legs rolled around her thighs into the shallows. Ahead of her the surface rippled, and something knifed through, heading into the tangled leaves on the pond's edge. "Snake!" I called out to her. "Be careful." She called back to me, "Don't worry, *chú*, they're water snakes." She went ahead, plucking the pods in a hurry and tossing them into a paper bag. The feathery leaves trembled as the black snake slithered out and cocked its head, watching. She stared at the snake, then hurled a bull nut at it. The snake dipped its head and retreated into the dark mass of diamond-shaped leaves.

"You make necklaces with these? And sell them?" I asked.

"No." She shook her head. "I can't tell you."

5

The helping girl hadn't been at the inn for three days.

It was midmorning when I came to her hut and found her lying wrapped in a blanket on her cot. She said she had bouts of diarrhea followed by a fever. She'd thrown up in bed. Her father had ground beefsteak leaves with garlic, mixed them with rice liquor, and made her drink. The fever didn't come down, the diarrhea didn't stop.

I looked at her tongue. Blackened. I took off her shawl and dabbed her perspiring forehead.

"It's some fish I ate three days ago," she said in a thin voice. "Daddy caught them. They were probably polluted by chemicals from the shrimp farms."

"Your dad won't be back until late today," I said, looking down at her blistered lips. "You need to go to the hospital."

"Am I going to die?"

"No, silly."

"I'm cold, *chú*."

I stood up. "Okay, I'll be back shortly."

The doctor at the town hospital diagnosed typhoid and treated her with antibiotics. He injected syringe after syringe of sodium solution. I came back the next day while she convalesced. She looked thinner. I held her hand. I knew how close to death she had been.

"I brought you soymilk," I said.

I removed the brown bag and gave her a glass jar of fresh soymilk. She held it, her cheeks flushed from the heat inside the small room. "Can I drink it, *chú?*" she said and then wet her dry lips.

"Sure. It's good for you."

She sat up. I handed her a glass and watched her drain it down, not wasting a drop. Still holding the empty glass in her hand, she looked at me, then at the unlit cigarette between my fingers. "Why don't you light it, *chú?*"

"I'd rather not," I said and put it back in my shirt pocket. "The smoke will make you cough."

"Am I going home today?"

Home. Her father was like a guest in their house. Before I could answer, someone paused at the door momentarily, then came into the room. I shook hands with the doctor and said I was grateful. The doctor glanced at the chart hung on the bedpost and said the girl was improving enough to leave the hospital the next day. I thanked him, and he left. She said her abdomen still hurt as she turned on her side to put the glass back on the table. The burn scar on her cheek shone in the table lamplight.

"Did you burn yourself?" I asked, pointing at my own cheek.

She squinted her eyes at me. I leaned back in the chair under her gaze and shrugged.

"I didn't burn myself," she said finally. "Mom did."

"By accident?"

"She didn't like the fish soup I cooked. She said . . ." The girl paused and touched her cheek where the burn was. "She said *Why don't you and your dad eat this?* and she threw the bowl in my face."

"Hell," I said, shaking my head.

"*Chú,*" she said, leaning forward to hand me the jar, "don't you want a sip of soymilk?"

"I'm not thirsty. It's for you."

She sat back. "Who brought you cigarettes now?"

"I did. I went to town."

"I'll be back to work tomorrow."

"Take another day's rest. You said your abdomen still hurts."

"It's tolerable now, not like a couple days ago. It hurt so bad then, I had tears in my eyes." She was stopped by a sudden cough. "But I'm feeling much better now. I want to go home and check on Daddy. Does he know where I am, *chú*?"

"Certainly. Did he drop by while I wasn't here?"

"I don't know. He might have before sunrise. He goes to sea very early. I must have been sleeping when he came. Or maybe the inn owner was here."

I looked away, hearing her wishful voice. Then she said, "I could've died, the doctor told me."

"Well." I tried to smile. "You're a good girl. You can't die."

"I almost died last summer."

"How?"

"I got bit by a rabid dog one night when I left the lodging house. This hospital didn't have vaccine. Said it was on back order. Daddy took me back. At dawn Daddy took me on a bus to the city. I was feverish. The city doctor vaccinated me. We arrived at our hamlet at dusk. Someone was waiting at the bus stop. It wasn't Mom. It was the inn owner."

6

"Look here."

I gave Cam a grass ball I had picked up from a hollow in the beach sand. She weighed it in her hand, a tennis ball made of sticks and grass and seaweed. "I've seen them before, *chú*," she said, tightening her headscarf because of the wind. "Daddy said the waves roll them together and the wind blows them up the shore."

The grass blades bend and dip, drawing their tips in the sand. Arcs and circles. She said arcs foretold stormy weather, and circles fair weather. I asked what lay in a depression between the dunes. The girl said vines, sometimes cranberry, sometimes bayberry. Densely clad, they carpeted the hollows in shining green.

On the wet sand, there were shore birds' footprints. As Cam stood back watching the sun set, I followed the birds' tracks down the beach until I saw ahead of me a flock of sandpipers—tan-colored, white-breasted—running with the waves. Twilight now. They were still hunting for food, probing every spot of sand, every ripple mark for mollusks. When they saw me, they scooted up the beach in quick-moving silhouettes. I followed their tracks until they were washed over by the waves. Alone on the sand stood a sandpiper in a pool of water. Sunset made red glimmers in the pool. The bird looked out over the sea and gave a lonely cry.

We went back to her hut, past the fenced-in garden plot, where sand drift had strangled most of the vegetation.

It was my last visit. Cam hadn't talked much since I told her. I sat down on the rickety chair while she stood at the table slicing a lemon. It would be a hot day tomorrow, she said. Cam always made a fresh jug of lemonade whenever she came to the inn in the morning.

"I'm going back to America tomorrow," I said.

There was a silence.

A sudden cry from Cam. I looked up. She had dropped the knife and was clutching her hand.

"You cut yourself?" I asked.

She balled her hand and blood was dripping. I grabbed an already squeezed lemon wedge and packed it around her cut finger. After a while I wrapped the cut with gauze.

She bit her lips, hard, looking toward the door. "I wonder what I can do tomorrow," she said to no one.

I looked at her. She lifted her face but kept her gaze at something over my shoulder.

"What d'you want to do?" I asked her.

"I don't know, *chú*."

I crimped my lips, looking around. "We can make something. Anything. I'll be gone soon. Well."

"I have something in my room." Suddenly she stopped with a shrug.

"What?"

"No." She shook her head emphatically.

Before I left, Cam said, "*Chú*, wait." She hurried into a corner, and when she came back out she gave me something wrapped in an old newspaper. I unwrapped it. A necklace made of bull nuts. Those glossy black bull nuts she picked from the pond. I felt them.

"For your girlfriend," she said, biting her fingernail.

"You made this?" I said, remembering that she'd refused to tell me what she picked them for.

She nodded.

"Thank you, Cam."

She shook her head as if in denial of hearing her name.

I wanted to hug her, but she stepped back and ran to the back of the hut. I called out to her. I could hear her voice, "I hate you, *chú*."

Outside, it was dark. When I looked back, I saw her standing in the door, just a blurred shadow. Then, I turned and walked away.

All the Pretty Little Horses

1

Mama, I died once as a stillbirth but was reborn as your son. By dying, as Saint Francis of Assisi said, we are born to eternal life.

The nurse said she would wash the baby, as the doctor removed his latex gloves. The doctor patted Papa on the shoulder and said, "I'm sorry." After he left, the nurse brought the baby to the bed and placed him in your arms. The baby was wrapped in a small blanket. In a hushed voice, the nurse said she would be back for him.

The baby looked as though he were asleep in the cradle of your arms. You were sitting up on the bed, your back cushioned by a pillow against the head railing. You bent your head to look at the baby's face, then parted a corner of the blanket to look at his limbs. Slowly you touched his nose, his closed eyes, his tiny mouth, trailing your fingers along his jawline. Gently, you pulled the blanket over his chest as if to keep him warm. With one arm cradling him, you freed the other and peeled back his pom-pom cap. He had dark hair in thin curly wisps. You caressed his pate, then combed his hair with your nails, brushing it back and forth like fingers strumming guitar strings. You tilted your face to one side to gaze at the baby. You held your gaze like that without moving your head, and you kept gazing at him, waiting for a miracle to breathe life into this stillbirth. After some time, you broke your gaze and dipped your head to kiss him on the brow. You pressed your lips against it, not moving, in that eternity. Quietly you cried.

Papa leaned over the bed to hug you.

"Do you want to hold him?" you said.

Yes, Papa wanted to. This tiny thing. Brownish. Dry chafed skin. Smelling of antiseptic. Still warm. His small mouth was red without the fine curves of the lips. His tiny hands clenched. He had fingernails, too, and his hands felt soft. Papa said, "So this is you who kicked and turned and moved around playing hide-and-seek in Mama's tummy. Did you hear Mama and Papa talking to you then? Did you hear Mama sing?"

He kissed the baby on the forehead. His skin no longer felt warm. Watery discharge was seeping from his nose and the corners of his mouth. The nurse came back. She asked to take the baby away. "I'm sorry, sir," she said. She wrapped the baby up in his blanket, and, Mama, you said you would like to hold him for the last time. Then, holding him in the crook of your arms, you rocked him gently, and you kept on rocking him as tenderly as a mother would rock her baby to sleep, until the nurse held out her hands. You shook your head. Your lips parted, but no words came out, and the nurse touched you on the elbow.

"I must take him away," the nurse said. She stroked your hands until they yielded, and the baby was back in the nurse's arms, tucked neatly in his blanket, the knitted cap pulled down to cover his brow. The nurse said goodbye and left the room with him, and the door clicked shut.

In the night came the sound of a baby crying. Perhaps just born.

2

You had insomnia, Mama, during your pregnancy. You could sleep only after a few glasses of wine. The insomnia got worse after the stillbirth. You couldn't sleep at night. The piano you played downstairs would wake Papa in bed. You would sing, *Go to sleep, baby child, Hush-a-bye, don't you cry. When you wake, you shall have, All the pretty little horses.* Late at night, a bottle of gin would bring you back to bed. At dawn, the sandman would come to take you to dreamland.

Papa worried about biochemical imbalances in the brain. The doctors suggested a lamp with a bluish luminosity. Rainy days and wintry weather made Papa fret. Did she have enough light? Would she stay balanced? He grew accustomed to seeing the lamp glowing blue, but still there was too much darkness.

Papa stayed up late in bed one night, reading a CIA briefing. The program waiting for him in South Vietnam nagged at him. He wasn't a man for myths and abstractions, so he realized the scope of the proposition the agency asked of him. He was to develop a pacification program to train the Army of the Republic of Vietnam to defend South Vietnam against the Viet Cong and the North Vietnamese communists. The agency gave him time to bring himself up to speed with the fledgling program. Also, he was to learn the language. "If you speak their language," the director said to Papa, "the Vietnamese will treat you like a family member."

Papa read until his eyes grew weary. Lying beside him, you needlepointed a stocking. Occasionally, you glanced up at the black-and-white TV. Papa finally put the papers back in his attaché and got in between the sheets.

"Can you turn off the light?" he asked.

You clicked the lamp off. Papa turned on his side away from the glare of the TV. You held the stocking in your lap, needles in your hands. Could you finish it by Christmas? This stocking showed a little boy with sugarplums hovering in his thoughts, sitting under a white pine. You wanted to leave a memory under the Christmas tree. For the lost child.

Soon Papa began snoring. Your eyes followed the scenes on the screen, your thoughts returning to what Papa had said about his duty in South Vietnam. How long this time? You cried when he was sent to Nam the first time. But you had managed on your own.

The man kissed the woman on the screen. Back then you would long for him on nights you couldn't sleep. A woman's longings opened a new realm of sensuousness. You discovered pleasures you only heard whispered about in girlhood. In those moments you imagined his body.

On the TV screen the woman broke away from the man, lit a cigar for him. The man puffed on his cigar as the match flickered. He gripped both her wrists, steadying her hands, and the match burned down to her fingers. She tried to look calm.

You turned off the TV but still saw the man gripping the woman's wrists. In the dark the images stirred your imagination. You turned on your back, felt dry in your mouth. Your body wasn't ready for bed. It felt warm, though you hadn't touched a drink this night. You turned to Papa, placed your hand on his hip. His breathing was shallow; his snoring stopped. You ran your hand along the curve of his hip, his thigh, but stopped as Papa woke. He turned toward you. He smelled of fresh linen, eyes blinking from half dreams. You touched his chest, unbuttoned his top. He followed your hands with his. You bent over him, your hair covering your face, his hands on your hips. He was still half in his dream, half in you when his desire peaked. You clutched his shoulders, your hair falling over his face. He said, "I'm sorry," as he stroked your shoulders. It had ended so soon, so abruptly. Your skin cooled. In Papa's arms you thought of the man in the movie and finally slept.

3

There was a walnut bookcase with glass doors framed by fluted columns, standing alone in a corner of our living room. It is still there, Mama. Papa stood in front of it. Do you believe in the afterworld? he asked himself. He didn't know how to answer that question as he gazed at the glass jar sitting on the top shelf. It was a plain jar capped with a green lid, inside of which were sand-colored ashes of his infant son.

"You have a son who came back from a stillbirth," a Chinese woman had told him. She was a Tarot and Runes reader who sat on a corner of K Street. Miss Thanh Hà, his Vietnamese-language teacher, had once asked him to consult the woman. Papa had chosen to avert his eyes from the glass jar every time he happened to pass by it. He had held that tiny baby, his skin still warm from his mother's womb, until it grew cold and his nose, his tiny mouth began secreting runny discharge. *Do you believe in the afterworld?*

The Chinese woman was there that afternoon when Papa left the Vietnamese language class. Miss Thanh Hà's replacement was a Vietnamese man in his late forties who spoke Vietnamese with a southern accent that threw off Papa. He couldn't sit in the class anymore; he couldn't bear looking at the chalkboard, at her handwriting still left in a corner. *Tôi mong gặp lại anh.* I hope to see you again. His temples ached. He had gone through all this again—reading, writing, listening—like an automaton, only it wasn't her. And that morning he sensed his hopelessness. When Papa walked to the corner to his car, he sensed it without any rationalization. The Chinese woman nodded at him, and he stopped. *Why don't you give it a try?* Miss Thanh Hà had said to him on one windy afternoon.

"Where is your friend today?" the Chinese woman asked.

"She's somewhere else," Papa said.

"Can I read for you today?"

Papa hesitated. The woman had a gentle smile, which wrinkled the corners of her mouth. Papa agreed. He picked the Runes, and she asked him to think on an issue. Then she gave Papa a velvet pouch, and he slipped his hand in and felt the pieces in it. They clanked, bone-dry, smooth to the touch. He pulled them out one by one and stopped after the fifth. She laid them vertically on a piece of cardboard on the ground. They looked like white pebbles, worn and washed into their own round-edged, rectangular shape. The final Rune he drew was a blank Rune. "You have a grave situation that has been with you," she said. "You must let it go. And let go also of your deepest guilt."

4

The first time I met Miss Thanh Hà, it was in Papa's class. It was a summer morning. There was water damage in the quadrant where I worked as a summer intern at the State Department, and I was told to go home. Papa said to me, "Nicola, you're welcome to sit in my class if you want. And learn Vietnamese."

Papa thought Miss Thanh Hà had the most beautiful eyes. They were serene, elongated. She was twenty-four years old, six years older than me at that time. It was a spring morning, airy and cool, in nineteen sixty-three, when she walked into the classroom.

She wrote her name on the blackboard in neat cursive letters, then added an accent over the "a" in her first name.

"Now 'Thanh' is my middle name. 'Hà' is my first name. In Vietnamese, a person's name has a meaning." She underlined her name, then wrote below it: *blue river*.

Everyone mouthed the words. She touched her hair, its lustrous black matching her eyes. She wore a rose-colored blouse of stretched batiste. Her face seemed flush, the color of her blouse.

"Do American names have meanings?" she asked.

Someone said yes with a shrug. Papa smiled. "Do they?" she asked him.

"Oh, sure," he said. "My last name is Rossi. It means 'red-haired person' in Italian."

She glanced at Papa's dark hair, standing in front of him. Not tall, perhaps five feet three inches. She asked everyone to introduce themselves and to tell the reason why they wished to learn Vietnamese. All six men, other than Papa, came from the State Department and worked for the Agency for International Development. Papa listened to them giving the same explanation: to help the South Vietnamese officials develop a Vietnamese civil administration as one of the goals of their civilian program. His turn came. Papa said, "I work for The Central Intelligence Agency. CIA or AID, we're all in the same boat. What we'll try to do in Vietnam is to improve our pacification program. We don't want to see our supplies reach the other shore and find out the war was over." Papa paused, scratching his head. "Maybe it'll work out better if I can speak to the *VeetCon* in their own language."

The men laughed. Miss Thanh Hà held Papa's gaze. Her almond-shaped eyes, liquid brown, examined him calmly.

"If you do want to speak to them in their own language," she said, "then speak the tones correctly. Unless you master the tones, you won't go very far in learning Vietnamese. It's a tonal language. The meaning of a word is pitch-controlled. Is this a challenge for you?"

"Well," Papa said, and heads turned toward him.

"Yes?" Miss Thanh Hà asked.

"When are you going to speak Vietnamese with the class?"

"On this very first day," she said. "The more you speak a language, the more you can learn its texture. Most importantly, it gives you confidence. But first, you must be determined, like a skater who refuses to grab the sill cap." She paused. "Can you do that?"

Everyone nodded. Papa flipped through the spiral-bound book, its pages scattered with words that had diacritical marks all over them. When he went to Nam a year before, he realized that the Vietnamese language made use of the English alphabet. Not unintelligible symbols, like Chinese. It looked like English—except for those odd little marks that seemed to crowd each word on the page.

"Today we'll learn the tones," Miss Thanh Hà said. "There are six tones in speaking Vietnamese. You can see from your textbook the accent marks that you find in French and German, except that Vietnamese language also has compound accents. The tone diacritics are placed above vowels in the syllables and also below in the case of the underdot."

She paused to pick up the textbook and started speaking in Vietnamese. Papa tried to follow its English translation. He was looking at the word "ma" with its accented variations: *má, mà, mả, mã, mạ.*

Miss Thanh Hà pronounced the word each time with a slight tonal change for each accented word. She turned to the blackboard and wrote the word "ma," then with a half turn to the class, said, "The Vietnamese vocabulary is built from the root word—like this one." She tapped the chalk on the word "*ma*" and said, "With six different pitches, it produces six different meaningful words, but that's not true in every case. Now, say *ma.*"

Everyone said it.

"*Ma*: ghost," she said, pointing at the explanation in the textbook. "*Má*: cheek." She wrote the word and added the acute accent with a flick of her wrist. "*Dấu sắc*, acute accent, rising pitch." She pushed her index finger upward on a slant. "*Mà*, but, *dấu huyền*, grave accent, falling pitch. *Mả*: tomb, *dấu hỏi*, half-rising pitch. *Mã*: horse, *dấu ngã*, half-rising pitch with a trailing echo. *Mạ*: rice seedling, *dấu nặng*, dropping pitch, heavily low." She made the class chant those words like a prayer.

Papa, forming words with his lips at first, joined the rest of the class. She made them say *ba, bá, bà, bả, bã, bạ,* then *me, mé, mè, mẻ, mẽ, mẹ.* After the drill, she said, "Say the word right, then you'll be in good rapport with a Vietnamese. Say the word wrong, you could offend a Vietnamese at a wrong time, depending on the meaning of the word and the context it's in. So, speaking the tone correctly is more than important—it's a must. On the other hand, the Vietnamese grammar isn't as rigid as French grammar, because there're no verb conjugations, no plurals, no articles, no masculine nor feminine form, and verbs don't change because of subject or tense."

Miss Thanh Hà put the chalk back on the base ledge of the blackboard and, smiling, turned to face the class. "That is good news to everyone, isn't it? Those here who know French would agree with me that conjugating verbs in French is hard. But it isn't so with Vietnamese grammar. Only speaking the language is difficult. Stress and intonation. You must speak each word clearly, because Vietnamese language is monosyllabic. Each word is a syllable, each word is short. So, do not speak fast."

Papa held her face in his gaze until she glanced at him. He blinked. He straightened his back, dropped his forearm that had propped the side of his face. His cheek still warm from resting against his forearm, he looked down at his textbook, wishing she would continue speaking so he could watch her: the way her lips formed words, how her eyes squinted, how she cocked her hip and pursed her lips when someone asked a question.

Miss Thanh Hà made every student repeat the same word to her satisfaction. Papa felt embarrassed saying those foreign words, which made no sense to him, and the harder he tried to correct his intonation the funnier it sounded. He had the hardest time pronouncing "đu đủ," the papaya. "Doo-dọo." He dropped low on the second word.

Giggling, Miss Thanh Hà covered her mouth and looked up at the ceiling. "If you ask for a papaya from a Vietnamese woman," she said, "your pronunciation will certainly get you in trouble."

Papa rolled his eyes. "Why?"

Miss Thanh Hà bit down on her lower lip to stop giggling and turned away. Finally, she said, "The way you pronounced it could mean . . . sexual intercourse. But it's a vulgar word for it."

The class broke out laughing. He shook his head. Those little accent marks, those short little words suddenly looked detestable like the Viet Cong's pith helmet. When the class was over, he closed the textbook.

Miss Thanh Hà asked everyone to study Chapter Two at home and practice greetings before the next class. "Vietnamese greetings adopt kinship terms and titles of respect," she said, putting her classroom materials into her briefcase. "And in greetings, your first name will be addressed. In Chapter Two, you'll see how different a Vietnamese name is arranged in comparison with an English name. The family name comes first, then middle name, then first name."

Papa shook his head.

Miss Thanh Hà looked amused at his distress. "Your name," she said, "will be Rossi Samuel in Vietnamese, and a Vietnamese will address you as 'Mister Samuel.' They go by the first name with a title of respect or a kinship term, like 'Aunt.' But all that will be for tomorrow." She turned around and wrote on the board, *Tôi mong gặp lại anh*, and underlined it. "I hope to see you again," she said, clicking shut her brief-case. "Good night, everyone."

Everyone filed out, each saying good night to her while she stood behind her desk. Papa remained seated. Now that the ordeal was over, he felt a pinch in his stomach, being alone with her. He had felt it when she first walked into the class-room, fresh in her rose-colored blouse, elegant with her ra-ven-black hair cut sharp on a slant. Now, he rose from the chair, pushing himself up, with his attaché still lying cross-wise on the writing tablet.

Miss Thanh Hà tilted her head. "Well, Mister Rossi."

"I'm not sure I'm made out for foreign languages," Papa said.

"You're made out to be a fighter."

"I appreciate your patience." Papa didn't want to leave yet. "Where do you live?"

"Kensington, Maryland."

"You drive?"

She shook her head. "I don't have a car." She glanced at his attaché still on the tablet arm. "And where do you live, Mister Rossi?"

"Call me Sam. I live in Gaithersburg, Maryland." Papa could see she didn't recognize the name. "I'm north of Kens-ington. Maybe I can give you a ride home, if you would like."

"For a change, yes," she said. "I lose patience waiting for the bus sometimes."

"You? Losing patience?"

She followed him to the car. He thought she had a

charming smile. She complimented him on his vehicle, a two-door Pontiac Grand Prix with white-walled tires, long slick fenders, and wood-grained steering wheel.

"A hefty car," Miss Thanh Hà said as she climbed onto the passenger seat. Papa stood at the passenger door and stole a quick look at her profile. He could see her blink. He cleared his throat and quickly walked around the front of his car.

"I know you don't have cars this big over there," Papa said, starting the engine.

"No, not in Vietnam. You don't see boat-sized cars like this. Have you been to Vietnam?"

"Yes. Over a year ago. And they didn't have oatmeal for breakfast."

"We have croissants, from French bakeries."

Papa had tried the croissants but missed the good old-fashioned donuts. He drove onto Connecticut Avenue, crossing K Street heading north. The sun was glaring through the windshield, so he reached up and flipped open the passenger visor.

"Thank you," she said.

"You can put your briefcase on the floor."

She was holding it in her lap. Papa glanced at her as she hunched slightly forward to place her briefcase on the car floor. The harsh light made him squint as her hand came up and opened the driver visor.

Papa never used the visor or sunglasses. He disliked them.

"The streets here are wide," she said.

"That's why we have big cars."

"Is this new?"

"This car? I bought it after I came back from Vietnam."
Papa drove with one hand on the steering wheel and smoothed his hair with the other.

When the light turned green, he stepped on the gas, and the car shot through the intersection. Out the corner of his eye, Papa could see Miss Thanh Hà, pushed back against the seat. His face felt hot from the blazing sun.

"What'd you think of the class?" he said.

"It's a good group. We'll be moving along well."

"I wish I could."

"Have faith."

"In whom?"

Miss Thanh Hà giggled.

"I have plenty of faith in myself," Papa said.

"Use it. Or borrow from mine. I never lose faith in my students."

"I'm too old for this."

"I've heard that before." Miss Thanh Hà paused. "You don't look that old."

"I have a son," Papa said. "He's eighteen."

"Do you have other children?"

"No, just one."

"And how long have you been married?"

"Twenty-five years."

"I admire people who have a long-lasting marriage."

He half turned to her. "Are you single?"

"Yes."

The silence that followed made Papa feel naked. He said nothing. He thought back twenty years, Mama, when you miscarried and then turned to drink. Two years later I was born. And those years that followed, your sickness in those long years.

"What did you do in South Vietnam?" Miss Thanh Hà asked.

"I was with a civilian program. A pacification program." Papa refrained from using the name.

"What does that mean?"

"Win the trust of the common people, win their support before the *VeetCon* get to them completely."

"That sounds ambitious. And what role may I ask do you play in it?"

"I had people working for me . . . ." Papa eased the car to a gentle stop at a light. He never talked about what he did in Nam.

"May I ask another personal question, Miss?"

"Go ahead."

"What part of *Veetnam* are you from?"

"My parents are from the north. I was raised in the North, then went South after nineteen fifty-four."

Papa thought of the First Indochina War, French War as called by the Vietnamese.

"So, you were a teenager when you left the North?"

"I was fifteen."

"Have you been here long?"

"Less than a year."

"You came for the job?"

"Not this job."

Papa accelerated through the stop-and-go traffic.

"I was an interpreter at the State Department," Miss Thanh Hà said. "I was working with AID. I have a bachelor's degree in linguistics. I want to work in the States, so I took a chance when they offered me a temporary position."

"As an interpreter at AID?"

"Only for three months—no contract."

"How's the pay of your teaching job?"

"Low," she said, glancing at him. "They pay for my room and give me sixty dollars per week."

Papa grunted. "Isn't much, is it?"

"Then, I met a French girl who came here the same time as I did. She was teaching French at this school. They offered her a contract, paid her five-hundred dollars a month plus per diem money."

"Was she also working for AID?"

"Both of us."

"Why the difference?"

"I don't have a clue," Miss Thanh Hà said, sighing. "I've been fighting to get this resolved, and if I'm lucky, I'll get backpay."

Papa stopped the car at the next red light. He turned to look at her. "Miss," he said, "you have every right to claim what belongs to you. I'll be happy to assist in your affair, if that would help."

Miss Thanh Hà dropped her gaze, lacing her hands in her

lap.

"Don't take it wrong," he said. "I don't interfere in people's lives unless I'm asked."

"I appreciate your concern, thank you."

Papa didn't know what Miss Thanh Hà thought, so he kept his eyes on the road. The air smelled clean, fresh, tinged with a trace of perfume. They entered the town's limits and passed a concrete slab erected on the roadside. Its weather-worn inscription read, *Welcome to Old Town Kensington*. She told him to turn onto a side street. The traffic thinned out on the quiet street that dipped and rose, shaded with tall maples and tulips and elms. She told him to stop in front of a white-painted frame house, its front porch shadowed by the crowns of oaks. He got out and walked around to the passenger side. She thanked him as he opened the door, and she eased herself out of the passenger seat.

"Do you live here by yourself?" Papa asked.

"No, I have two roommates."

"Girls?"

"Yes, French girls. One got the contract from AID that I told you about." Miss Thanh Hà looked toward the house then back at him. "Thank you for the ride."

"My pleasure." Papa walked back to the driver's side, carrying with him the imprint of her eyes. He checked the rearview mirror as he was moving out from the curb. She was walking back toward him. He stopped. She rested her hand on the passenger door and peered at him.

"May I take you up on your offer to help?" she said.

"Of course. I'll look into it. I promise."

She stood back as he drove off.

5

It had been a month since that first class, and Papa still had trouble pronouncing Miss Thanh Hà's last name, among other words. Nguyễn Thanh Hà. Not *Nu-gen*, she'd told him. Not *Gwen*. Raise your pitch, one smooth enunciation. Papa practiced until his mouth felt dry, at times plugging one ear to hear himself better, feeling silly at the sounds he made. He had brought home the cassette tapes to listen to the word pronunciations, and every night he'd spend an hour in his den recording his own sounds to mimic the voice on the tapes. "Your jaws must relax," she'd said. "Let your lips form the sounds." Papa would let me speak into the recorder, and those Vietnamese words came back out in my voice just like the man's voice on the tape.

"Maybe you should take my place," he said.

"Papa, you can't learn a language if you don't like it."

"It wasn't my choice to learn Vietnamese."

"Then don't hold anything against it."

The second time I sat in Miss Thanh Hà's class happened on the day I had a job interview at one o'clock in the afternoon. Papa told me to sit in his class, since the interview office was in a building nearby.

That morning, Miss Thanh Hà had read a textbook story to the class in Vietnamese: *The Dragon and the Immortal*, or *Tiên Rồng*, from whom the Vietnamese claimed their lineage.

Miss Thanh Hà made everyone in the class read it out loud in Vietnamese, everyone except me. She would occasionally correct a wrong pronunciation and at times, nodding, compliment a student. Papa waited his turn, crossing his legs now and then. Something told him that Miss Thanh Hà was giving him time to listen, so when his turn came, he would have a better feel for the language.

She glanced at her watch. Noon.

"We take a recess," Miss Thanh Hà said. "Let's meet again at one."

She waited as the class filed out. She stood, in her smooth orange crush silk blouse, its ruffled cuffs a pale yellow matching the tone of its eyelet-embroidered collar. She took a step toward me.

"How do you like our class?" she asked, smiling.

"I think I'll take up Vietnamese in college," I said, rising from my chair.

"Is that a compliment?"

"Well, if they offer it."

She laughed. A head taller than Miss Thanh Hà, I stood in front of her, slightly bent, feeling awkward. Papa had a look like an outsider. She turned to him.

"I'd like to talk to you privately," she said.

He told me to go and have lunch. Then Papa walked out of the building with her. The sunlight was harsh after the passing clouds, and as they walked up the street she put on her sunglasses.

"A beautiful day," she said.

"Thanks for sparing me in the class," Papa said. "I know I'd sound like an idiot reading those words out loud."

"That's not what I want to speak to you about privately," she said. "I wish to thank you . . . ."

"Thank me?"

"AID has agreed to give me backpay and a contract," she said. "I thought my petition was futile, until you intervened."

"That's how the justice system works in our country." Smiling, Papa nodded. "Well, you might have to bend it sometimes."

"Thank you. I need a friend in this country."

"Would you like to have lunch somewhere?" Papa said.

She gave him a sidelong look and a tiny star of sunlight glinted on her shades.

"I must ask you an enormous favor," she said. "Can you show me around town?"

Before he could say yes, she said, "I've been in Washington, DC, for almost a year now, and I haven't got a chance to see it."

Papa pointed to a deli at the corner. "We can grab a sandwich and be on our way."

Miss Thanh Hà ate only an apple for lunch, so Papa changed his mind and ordered a toasted bagel and black coffee. The sun was in his eyes as he drove out of the garage, and her face was shaded by the passenger visor.

"It doesn't seem like anyone has ridden in your car since I did," she said.

"How'd you know that?"

Her hand, clutching the red apple, reached up to touch the visor. "I remember the angle you left it on."

He washed down his mouthful with a sip of coffee, then motioned with his head at the downtown scenery. "Where to, Miss?"

"I want to see Washington, DC. Just a quick tour through your eyes."

"Through my eyes, huh?"

Papa cranked open the window, the wind roaring, whipping his tie around his neck. He swept his hand toward the glass-box buildings on the other side of the median.

"This K Street," he said, "used to be one of the finest residential quarters in the city. Now it's all gone."

Miss Thanh Hà looked out the car window.

"I used to work after school in a department store on K Street," Papa said, "where my mother was a sewing girl. I used to carry boxes of garments around like a human conveyor belt."

"I wasn't even born then."

Papa felt sober hearing that.

At the next intersection, of K Street and Connecticut Avenue, Papa turned right on Seventeenth Street, heading toward the Potomac River. While they waited on a red light at Constitution Avenue, he pointed at a stone house on the opposite corner. "That house used to be the lockkeeper's house."

"What is a lockkeeper?"

He told her.

"The Washington Canal used to run by the front of a market about here, the whole length of what's now Constitution Avenue, and boats carrying fresh produce would come down the canal and unload at the market. I remember seeing a Chinese coolie drop dead here, right at the dock."

She turned to look at him.

"He was carrying a crate on his back when he collapsed. My mother came to his side. He was already dead, bleeding from his mouth and his nose. Tuberculosis."

Miss Thanh Hà took off her sunglasses. Papa drove north on Seventh Street. Then she said, "I can't visualize what used to be here. Where I come from, things don't change that much."

"If you move around, then you lose touch with those changes. Have you moved a lot?"

"Some," she said. "I hardly had a place I could call my old town. I wish I could see a town the way you do. With memories, with little stories. Do you have a sense of belonging?"

"Always. I'd gone away once because of the war, but, even then, I felt I'd never left." Papa drank down his coffee. "So, you moved from North to South Vietnam?"

"Yes. Then shortly after we settled in South Vietnam, both my parents died. I was fifteen at that time and had no one else to turn to. An old French couple took me in."

"Who were they?"

"They knew my parents back in those days in North Vietnam. They were missionaries. I moved to Lyon to live with them."

Papa felt touched by this story. Left a widow, his mother had spent her life in a sweatshop. She was fifty when she died from stomach cancer. It was a horror to see her suffer during her final days. She would return his grip on her wrist by clutching his hand when he visited her each afternoon after work. She insisted that he should drop by only on the weekends, for it was a long drive to Georgetown from his military barracks in Virginia. He told her he had no one else in the world to care for, and she shook her head and said, "No, Sam, you have a family. Care for them. I'm doing fine. Other than this disease, I'm doing fine."

He hadn't felt for anything, for anyone, in a long time.

"Are you Catholic?" he asked.

"I'm Buddhist."

Papa couldn't imagine any religion without Jesus Christ and the Bible. He rarely went to church; only Mama did. Still, Papa considered himself a Presbyterian in honor of his family tradition. He had heard of Buddhism, but it was only another name to him.

Papa parked on Potomac Street, and they walked to the towpath along the canal. Giant sycamores and silver maples leaned over the path, their dappled leaves casting golden coins of light on the ground.

Miss Thanh Hà put on a hat. "My eyes are sensitive to strong sun," she said. "Without sunglasses, I have vertigo on a day like this."

Her English was formal, Papa thought.

"Such a pleasant view," she said, "to have a canal running through the heart of a town."

He told her that in summertime the National Park Rangers would reenact the historic past of the canal by inviting people to ride with them along the canal in a barge pulled by mules.

As they strolled, clouds gathered, dragging a long shadow across the ground and over the water. The wind picked up, rushing toward them down the towpath, and the surface of the water shuddered with tiny creases. The air felt crisp. Miss Thanh Hà hugged herself across her chest. Papa could see that the chill bothered her. He took off his jacket and draped it over her shoulders.

"Thank you," she said. "You're very kind."

"So, you can enjoy our walk," he said. "I might've asked you this before. Are you dating anyone?"

"Am I? No."

"You haven't met the right person?"

"You can say that."

The right person—Papa grinned, trying to hide his nervousness. He pointed toward the canal. "This is the historic site of Georgetown," he said. "It used to be a tobacco port.

Miss Thanh Hà, tugging at the rim of her lavender hat,

asked Papa, "Have you ever traveled on this canal?"

"When I was five, I rode on a barge with my mother, and we went as far as Cumberland. The night we approached Cumberland, my mother saw a ghost. Well, everyone on the barge did, except me. I was sleeping."

"So, you heard it from your mother then?"

"She told me it wasn't the first time that people saw this particular ghost. She said those who traveled on barges up and down the canal had seen it at night, and it always appeared on that bridge. She said it was the ghost of a headless Irishman and that bridge was the site of his murder."

Miss Thanh Hà pulled Papa's jacket around herself as they walked into the wind. "Do you believe in ghosts?" she said, gazing ahead.

"No, none of that stuff. Do you?"

"We believe in the afterlife."

"As a Buddhist?"

She nodded.

6

What Miss Thanh Hà said about the afterlife remained intriguing to Papa, and he kept thinking about it for days. He asked me if Buddhism believed in afterlife. I said, "I don't know. Why did you want to know, Papa?"

"Nothing important," he said.

"Does it have something to do with Miss Thanh Hà?"

"Why do you say that?"

"She's Buddhist."

"Yes, I know she's Buddhist."

"I know you care for her, Papa."

He lifted his face at me, then quickly looked away.

I had talked to Miss Thanh Hà a few times after the day I sat in her class. Sometimes I would drop in from the State Department during my lunch break. A few times, I lunched with Papa and her, and, twice, we walked a good length of Seventeenth Street, past the lockkeeper's house at Constitution Avenue and up to the Potomac River. Leaning against the guard rails on Kutz Memorial Bridge, we could see over the southern horizon a looming airplane on its ascent from the National Airport. Both times, we had to hurry back before our lunch breaks were over. Papa slowed his pace so she could keep up with us. There was a bench at a bus stop, and she sat down to catch her breath. Patiently, he waited with her but sent me back to my workplace. Papa wanted to be alone with her, I knew. He cared for her, a genuine feeling he could not deny.

Mama, that evening Papa came home to find you squatting on the floor, scooping the shards of glass one by one with your hand into a plastic bag. There were pieces of broken glass near the kitchen table. He stood, watching you brush the rest onto a dustpan.

"What happened?" Papa asked.

"I knocked over my glass of wine." You mopped the floor with a towel and wringed it repeatedly at the sink, letting the water run.

"Please stop," Papa said. Your obsession with cleanliness had tested his nerves before.

You sat down across from him with a fresh glass of wine. Papa ate dinner in silence, listening to the sounds of his own chewing and the clinking of his fork against knife. When I was there, I filled that vacuum, the space between you and him. When I wasn't there, Papa became aware of the emptiness.

In silence he ate, you and he like two strangers who happened to sit at the same table in a restaurant.

He swallowed his mouthful and stood up. "What's wrong?" you said.

"I need coffee."

"You and I need to talk."

Papa hated hearing you say that. He stood at the stove, where the air was warmed by the steam of the percolating coffee.

"What's that woman's name?"

"Who?"

"Don't you have an answer?"

"Yes, I have an answer. Her name is Thanh Hà." Papa never lied, but now he felt like a man on trial.

"I'm your wife." You took a small sip of wine. "Is she single?"

"She's single."

"Isn't she a Buddhist?"

"She's a Buddhist, like you're a Christian."

"I'm a baptized Christian."

Papa looked up at the ceiling.

"She's a heathen," you said. "Her Buddha wasn't baptized, was he?"

"How in the world do I know?"

"If she worships someone who's never been baptized, then what is she? A heathen. She's damned. That's what she is."

"Where did you get this idea from, Catherine?"

"It's a fact. Didn't you know?"

No, Papa didn't know. Neither did he know anything about the Buddha.

"Sam," you said. "Does she mean anything to you?"

"What on earth is this all about?"

"Please don't raise your voice at me."

Papa lifted the mug to drink, then stopped. He set it down on the kitchen countertop.

"Sam," you said again. "Answer me. Do you like her?"

"What am I supposed to say?" His face felt hot.

"Like a good Christian."

"I'm not going to answer that question."

"Because it's against your conscience?"

"Because I choose not to."

"Very good," you said, wiping the corners of your mouth. "How old is she?"

"Can we not talk about this?"

"Is she Nicola's age? Tell me. I want to hear you say it."

"You asked me what you already know?"

"She's only Nicola's age."

"Yes, you—"

"Don't say anymore."

Papa strode past you. "The evening is yours," he said.

"You must like her a lot, Sam. There's cologne on every shirt you've worn."

That spun Papa around. "You went through my—Jesus!"

You kept a neutral gaze. "Don't yell at me. I should be the one who's mad."

"Enough, Catherine."

"A man your age, twice her age—"

"I said, enough!"

"The weakness that every man has—"

Papa grabbed the bottle of wine. "Weakness—here, take it!"

He dropped it in your lap. The bottle rolled off and hit the floor with a dull thud.

Papa stared down at your face. In the light, your eyes were pale blue veined with red lines, your hair like blown-away straw.

"Go away," you said.

7

The sound of falling acorns on the roof would take Papa back to that night at Miss Thanh Hà's, the night he paid Miss Thanh Hà his last visit. Mama, you were screaming at him as he hurried out the door. "Whore, whore—damned whore!" Your words chased him as he drove through the pouring rain and found Miss Thanh Hà, outlined in yellow light, on the porch of her rented house. He dashed across the lawn to her. The porch light was dim, darkening her face. She had seen a ghost. The ghost of a person without a head standing by her bed. She was alone in the house, her French roommates away somewhere for the weekend.

"Do you want to go inside?" Papa asked.

"No."

They stood in silence. Rain blew wet pine needles onto the porch and hurled in silver sheets across the streetlights.

"Can we go for a ride?" Miss Thanh Hà said. "I can't stay here. I'm going out of my mind."

"Of course."

"Let me drive, please."

"Okay, if it will help."

Rain blew against the windshield, drumming on the roof. Papa told her to get off Connecticut Avenue and get on the Beltway toward Rockville. "Just drive. I'll let you know when to get off."

Miss Thanh Hà stared straight ahead, her profile white against the window glass. She said she wouldn't go back into the house. The sound of falling acorns had spooked her. Papa asked her where she would spend the night. In a hotel, she told him, until her roommates returned home. She asked Papa if he believed in the afterworld, and he remembered she had asked him that on the towpath.

"You ask me to dispute what you've seen?" Papa said. "Do you think the apparition was there or just part of your dream?"

"It was there," she said, gripping the wheel.

Water spattered the windshield as a rig carrying timbers overtook them on the outside lane. The car trembled when the rig roared by, cutting in front of them. Papa told her to move to the passing lane and not to trail the rig. She changed lanes, keeping behind a roadster that kicked up sprays of water in the headlights.

"I'm not superstitious," she said, squinting ahead, "but I believe that apparition appeared for a reason."

"What reason?"

"A foreboding. A sign."

"Of what?" Papa asked. "Please tell me. I want to know."

"A foreboding about me."

Papa's heart jumped hearing her say something so horrifying. He glanced at her, the highway lights reflected a dull amber on the rain-splashed windshield.

"Would it matter if I don't believe in the supernatural?" he finally said.

"If you don't, am I absurd in your eyes?"

Papa heard her tone: soft, distant. Yet, it stirred in him a sympathy. In that instant, he felt affection. A thought came to his mind, and it was a thought he had suppressed time and again.

"There's something I want to ask you," he said, staring ahead.

"Yes, Sam."

They were fast approaching the split when the roadster shot up alongside the rig to overtake it, speeding past its length of overhanging planks.

"I want to ask you about . . . ."

The roadster cut in front of the rig and across the inside lane toward an exit. The rig wailed, brakes shrieking, shuddering against its own load. Papa saw its rear end jagged with timbers as they crashed through the windshield on a slant, shattering the glass. The car stopped, slamming him forward, and his head punched through the windshield. Lights flashed on and off.

He felt raindrops on his one cheek, the other cheek pressed against the cold, wet metal of the hood. A tiny voice in his head cried out to him to wake. Lights blinked in his blurry vision. He strained his eyes to focus. A voice in his ears, *Jesus Christ, aww God, aww God Almighty, aww Jesus Christ* . . . . A man eased Papa away from the windshield. He kept asking Papa if he was all right. Papa felt the cold rain on his lips. He slumped on the dashboard. He turned toward the driver's seat. Blood, everywhere. A plank was jammed through the steering wheel, pinning a body. He could not see a head.

The Dream Catcher

From the bay window in Robert Fitch's living room, I saw the *xích lô* pedicab in the backyard, parked next to the shed, under an oak tree. At dusk, the white picket fence behind the *xích lô* blended with the snow thick on the ground.

A Vietnamese pedicab? What's it doing here? I hadn't expected to see a *xích lô* in the backyard of an American home.

A hand tapped me on the shoulder. A tall man with a goatee looked down at me. He smelled of tobacco and had a pipe the color of red wine stuck in his mouth. He looked in his late thirties. His blue eyes fixed me with a hard stare.

"Chào anh," he said in broken Vietnamese. Then, he leaned his head toward the *xích lô*. "Must be asking yourself how that baby got there, eh?"

The man switched his drink to his left hand, and his hand shot out to shake mine. "Gene Jensen," he said, "the other deputy."

Robert Fitch, the director of the Bureau of Refugee Programs at the State Department, had two deputy assistant secretaries: Vinh, my uncle, and Gene Jensen, Fitch's right-hand man. Both were vying for the director's job upon Fitch's imminent retirement.

I shook Gene Jensen's hand, which was as soft as a woman's but cold. "Minh Nguyen, public affairs officer."

"I've heard about you." Jensen shifted his gaze to the *xích lô*. "Three months ago, that baby was mine. Fitch got a kick out of it the first time he saw it in my backyard. So, I gave it to him."

"How did you get it?" I asked.

The doorbell rang. More guests entered the foyer, bringing the cold air in with them. Jensen raised his glass and waved at them.

I had seen my uncle's competitor chat with just about everybody at the party, like a politician looking for votes. His eyes never rested, while his hand kept stroking his reddish goatee.

"You know who was the very last one to ride in that pedicab before it went into retirement?" Jensen said louder above the drone of people's voices. "I was. Before that, uh, *phu xích lô*—I mean the pedicab coolie—dropped dead in front of my eyes. It was unbelievable. He was taking my twenty-*đồng* bill, and, before, I knew it, he started coughing up gobs of blood. Fell flat on his back. I chased his bill before the damned wind blew it away." He paused a moment to laugh at the notion. "When I came back, he was dead. Poor bastard had TB. I should've guessed it before I hopped into his pedicab. The tiny sucker was all bones with toothpick legs. I was surprised he was able to pedal me home."

Jensen sipped his drink, then clucked his tongue. "The police pulled his body to the curb just outside my house and put a poncho over him. After that it rained—I mean monsoon rain. Lucky for him he wasn't washed away by the time his friends came to claim the body. But I decided to keep that contraption before someone else pedaled it off. What you're looking at is a relic. So, when I was getting the hell out of Nam, I had it shipped back home with me."

I looked toward the dining room and, without looking at him, asked what he was doing in Vietnam.

"Serving my country."

"For how long?"

"One year. Went in sixty-eight, came home in sixty-nine. Got my first draft card in my senior year of high school. One-A. When I entered college, they sent me a revised draft card—three-A. But the Nam situation got worse, so my status reverted to one-A. Then, I got married, and they sent me another revised draft card. Back to three-A. They kept nipping at my rear end—not that I was trying to be one step ahead of them, but I wanted to finish college first. I graduated, but they changed my status back to One-A—married college student with no children."

While he was justifying himself, Jensen moved sideways to the dining room, nudging me along. The glare of the crystal chandelier caused my eyes to squint.

I had never been in such a beautifully furnished home. Antiques were everywhere, and the Fitches' valuable doll collection was more than simply toys.

The columned entrance to the dining room was draped with a pine swag dotted with snowflakes, dried pinecones, deep blue magnolias, and red berries. While I refilled my glass with rum fruit punch, Jensen dropped some ice cubes into a glass and added Scotch.

Foods cluttered a dining table draped with a golden silk brocade. In the center stood a brass candelabrum. Mixed in with fresh fruits and vegetables were gold-sprayed gourds and hand-painted papier mâché pomegranates, apples, and pears. I glanced at a bowl of eggplant and red peppers, then looked again, not sure if they were real.

"What part of Nam are you from?" Jensen asked.

"Hue."

"Been there." Jensen dipped a breadstick into a sauce of chopped pistachios and olive oil. "First three months I was with an infantry unit that laid sensors along the Ho Chí Minh Trail in Ban Me Thuot. That helped us bomb the hell out of the VC who traveled that road. But Charlie got smart. They brought in antiaircraft and placed them where they thought our sensors were laid. From there, they shot down our planes. Right after that, I was transferred to Hue."

I helped myself to a slice of roasted chicken and a lump of rice stuffed inside a grape leaf. Jensen crunched on the breadstick. "Hue was a godforsaken land," he said. "It rained so much, I thought I'd have moss growing on my body. Seems all they grew out of that teeny-weeny strip of land was rice.

No wonder they're so small." He dropped his eyes on me. "Like you."

I caught malice in Jensen's eyes before the man blinked. He soaked another breadstick in the pistachio sauce and crunched it. It seemed he had found his favorite food, for he started stacking up breadsticks on his plate.

I headed back to the living room for fresh air.

Jensen trailed behind. "Tell you the truth, there wasn't much to do but shoot at the water buffalo for target practice from Highway One. That was the only thrill." He eyeballed me while working his tongue behind his teeth to pry something loose. "Those damned villages along that highway were VC villages. They operated right under our nose."

I glared at Jensen. I felt ill to know that Jensen was one of those US Marines who rumbled down Highway One, terrorizing the civilians with their malice. The marines called it the Avenue of Horror. A two-lane asphalt highway, heavy with US convoys, ran through Hue, crowded in on both sides by paddies and aluminum sheet-roofed houses.

I took a quick sip of my fruit punch. "I was thirteen in sixty-nine," I told Jensen, "and one day I heard this terrible news. From a US convoy on Highway One, an American GI threw a C-ration can at a Vietnamese boy riding a water buffalo in the nearby paddy. The boy was struck on the head and killed."

Jensen, nodding, mumbled through his mouthful, "Yeah, I rode in that truck."

I stared at him. He could have stabbed me and still not have hurt me as much as the tone of his voice did.

Even before I met Jensen, I had imagined him as snotty, obnoxious. That image was courtesy of my Uncle Vinh. "So, you rode in that truck," I said. "What did you do afterward?" I thought of him chasing a bill in the wind.

"Nothing." Jensen shrugged. "In wartime, shit happens. Let me tell you a little story. I was staying at Camp Eagle, not far from Highway One. One day about noon, the marines in the barracks caught a Vietnamese girl who worked as a cook at the base. The way she walked across the mess hall just didn't look right, like she was measuring her steps and figuring the distance between the mess hall and the adjoining hospital. The VC bastards needed those coordinates for their mortars. Well, the marines locked her up, cross-examined her, and by the time they were through, each man had taken turns fucking the shit out of her. After that, they jammed a flare up her vagina and popped it." He held my gaze and smiled contemptuously. "I could've been the sucker sitting in the latrine that night, right on the coordinates, and had my ass blown to pieces."

I rubbed my hands together to dry my sweating palms. A few people glanced our way. Some looked away as they caught my gaze.

Jensen belched. "What we did to them was nothing compared to what they did to us. Those assholes even booby-trapped children! A man in my unit picked up a crying baby left all by himself in a hooch. Before I could blink my goddamned eyes, I heard an explosion. Can you guess? A hand grenade had been strapped to the baby's back. Burst him open like a watermelon. My man lost his face completely—no nose, no eyes."

I felt a twinge in my gut. I wished I hadn't run into this hypocrite.

"Don't tell me you didn't know about their atrocities," Jensen said. "Those who didn't were liberals that should be hanged by the balls."

The man talked like an enlisted soldier willing to sacrifice for his country. Yet he had hitched up his pants to run away from Uncle Sam's reach, doing what he could to get those three-As on his draft card, so he wouldn't get his ass impaled in Nam by a VC's punji stick. And now he was telling me about the naiveté of the public toward the war.

"But naiveté wasn't what killed us, was it?" I said out of irritation. The roasted chicken began to taste so dry in my mouth, I had to wash it down with a gulp of fruit punch.

"No!" Jensen belched. "You South Vietnamese relied too

damned much on our support, that's all. You ever ask your-self how South Vietnam managed to keep its economy afloat during the war?" He paused. "US dollars. Your country lived on a life-support system and took its last breath when we pulled the plug in '72."

I turned to leave and saw Uncle Vinh and Dick Wolcott, the undersecretary, both listening to what Jensen had said.

Uncle swept his hand toward me. "Dick, my nephew."

Wolcott was Uncle's age, 48, but had a billowy cloud of white hair. He happened to be Fitch's boss and Uncle's men-tor. The two of them had been friends back in the sixties when Wolcott was an advisor to the Saigon mayor.

Wolcott pumped my hand.

"Dean Cohen says good things about you. He liked your general knowledge for a person your age."

His words cooled my temper. Wolcott and Uncle were heading toward the family room, from which I could hear the piano playing *"Auld Lang Syne."*

Feeling morose, I drifted out of the room. In the living room, a group of guests huddled in front of the television set, watching the Rose Bowl Parade in Pasadena.

I wandered into the library, its glass door ajar. The air in-side smelled of pipe tobacco and old leather. The dark wal-nut-paneled walls displayed a few paintings. Taking up one whole wall was a bookcase with a cherry finish. Through its glass panels, I saw the spines of hardbound books and some religious figurines in white glazed porcelain.

The door creaked behind me. A girl came in. She was pe-tite, with platinum hair cut in long strands to shape her oval face.

"Hi, Minh."

I had no recollection of our having met. She stepped up and gave me a plate with a wedge of cake on it.

"They just cut the cake, and your uncle was wondering where you were. I'm Denise Duvalier."

"You must be from the front office."

"Yes. I made up the guest list for this party."

I felt a flutter in my stomach. So, she was Fitch's secretary. She had included my name down on the guest list. Why? She hardly knew me.

She sipped her drink. It looked like whiskey. "How's the cake?"

It was moist with rum that seeped into my breath and straight to my head.

"Would you like some?" I offered it to her.

"No, thanks." She shook her head. "I hate sweets."

She raised her tumbler and took a sip.

"You don't like crowds, do you?" She glanced up, tasting her lips. Her skin was lightly freckled under her eyes—turquoise-blue eyes, too big for her small face.

"No, I don't," I said. "Look at this. Does Fitch have a sense of humor, or what?"

On a bookshelf sat a wicker basket lined with a black-and-white polka dot cloth blanket, and lounging in it were a father pig, a mother pig, and three piglets in bisque porcelain.

"Isn't that cute?" she said, then pointed at the nutcracker set. "But I like these."

The king and queen wooden nutcrackers wore jewels that glimmered on their hand-painted costumes.

"Must be real jewelry." She rested her forehead against the glass panels. She inhaled sharply, rubbing her hand on her throat as though she were feeling the gems resting there.

In one corner of the room sat an aquarium, glowing cerulean blue. The water pump whirred softly. Denise sat down in front of it, both legs folded under her in a yoga position. She looked at home. I sat down beside her.

"I'm jealous of you," she said. "D'you know that?"

I laughed. "I haven't the foggiest idea why."

"Looks like I might be working for your uncle soon."

I was tempted to ask where she had gotten that idea, but she quickly drained her whiskey and turned to me.

"You live with your uncle?" She knew the answer, nodded at the same time I did. "I guessed so. What about your family? Any of them here?"

"I'm my parents' only child," I said. "They're still in Vietnam."

"Sorry to hear that."

"Why?"

"Don't you wish they were here with you?"

"They decided to stay."

"Good Lord, why?"

"There's a Vietnamese idiom about the motherland. It may sound funny if I translate it."

She looked at me without blinking. "Go ahead."

"*Quê mẹ là nơi chôn nhau cắt rốn.*"

"Sounds nice."

"The Motherland is where we bury our placenta and sever our umbilical cord."

"I think I see," she said, nodding. "But that leaves you here all by yourself. Must've been a tough choice to make."

"No, they simply chose tradition. Like sweet wine to old age, you know."

A Persian cat meowed, rubbing its russet coat against Denise's thigh. She stroked the cat behind the ears.

"Oh, what do you want, cutie? I haven't seen you since you found a new home."

"Did he come from a humane society?"

"She. Queen's her name. She was a surprise gift that Jensen gave Fitch."

"What for?"

"Fitch's birthday last October. We all went to a restaurant except your uncle. I guess Vinh didn't care much for it. Jensen masterminded that luncheon and surprised the heck out of Fitch." She laughed. "Fitch was eating when he suddenly jumped up, yelling, 'What the hell is that?' He looked under the table, and so did everybody else. And this little cutie came out. Jensen picked her up. Then he read the tag on her collar. *My name is Queen. I was a cat without a master until you come along.*"

First a *xích lô*, then a Persian cat. This Jensen knows how to scratch his boss' itch.

"How long have you worked for Fitch?" I said.

"Been his personal secretary for six years, since high school." She closed her eyes as if she felt sleepy, then smiled. "I can relate to your parents and to those who got stuck in one place for the rest of their lives. People go through their midlife crisis at forty. That's when they've discovered their own limits. There's nothing left that they haven't already tried. Their wheels start spinning. When you look at them, you realize you're looking at yourself in a crystal ball. Dead stuck—most of us are." She sucked in her lower lip. "I'll need another drink."

She wobbled as she rose. I took the tumbler from her hand, stood, and went to refill it for her. Perturbed, I knew now why she had sought me out. I could sense her fear of becoming an old hag someday, doing the same thing with the same job. She was an opportunist who knew how to influence the roll of the dice.

When I came back with her Scotch, she was still sitting, a small figure glowing pale against the water's reflection. Again, I sat by her side.

Her eyes sought mine. "Do you have a sweetheart?"

"No."

"Waiting for the right person?"

I shrugged, trying to look enigmatic.

"Aren't you lonely?"

"No." I met her gaze. It was straight, steady, and quite unnerving.

"Minh, you're lying." She grinned. "Even when you're with someone, you still feel that loneliness."

I wasn't lonely, not really. I called it a mishap.

Denise was blessed, being an American and not an immigrant. She was blessed, not having to feel the mishap that held captive a man without roots. In that bleakness I knew I didn't feel lonely, because I didn't feel anything.

Denise's eyes were gazing at the aquarium. I wondered if she were chasing the ghosts of good times past.

Someone was playing the piano again. I recognized the

melody: "The Sting." Denise nodded to the tune, humming to herself. She raised her glass and downed it. She coughed, clasping the empty tumbler in her lap.

"How 'bout another drink?" I picked up her empty glass.

"No, thanks."

Up close, her face shimmered in the light. The platinum blond of her hair set off the crimson of her lips. She tried to stand. Her knee bumped against mine as she took hold of my hand. She lifted her face. Our lips touched. I sucked in my breath, feeling her mouth work on mine. Then, lips crimped, she cupped my face. "Can you drive me home?"

Denise opened her eyes. She looked down her chest, while stroking my hair. "You a virgin?" she said.

I wet my lips with a nod. Her pillow had the same scent of watermelon as her lipstick. The downy hair on her forearm tickled my neck. "Was that a guess?" I asked.

"No, I could tell." She mussed my hair. "You'll find out when you make love to a virgin girl."

I smiled and said nothing.

"You shook like a baby when you came," she said.

I flicked her nipple with my fingernail. She cringed, grabbed my hand. "But you're a good learner."

"You're a screamer."

"Both Kurt and I are screamers. I thought sometimes we woke our neighbors right in the middle of the night."

"Is he your boyfriend?"

"He'll be out of jail next month." She paused. "Larceny."

I felt something wrong when she said that. What type of girl was she?

"Just don't tell your uncle that you lost it to me, okay?" She chuckled.

Her chest heaved. Her perfumed skin, having perspired, felt cool against my cheek.

"Want to date an American girl?" she asked.

"How about dating a Vietnamese guy?"

"I know nothing about Asian cultures. My farthest trip from home was to San Diego. I'm a die-hard American. The only Chinese dish I can eat is fried rice."

"Why don't you go with me to this Vietnamese musical show next weekend?"

"What is it about? Is everything in Vietnamese?"

I sat up. Denise hugged herself to cover her chest.

"It's a Vietnamese musical variety show with traditional folk songs. Can't be in English."

"I know that." She pushed herself up on her elbows. "I would feel lost. I don't think I want to be there. But don't be offended. You want a drink?"

I shook my head. Denise walked barefoot into the kitchen. Outside, snowflakes fell in white dots across the streetlights. The wind hissed through a gap in the window.

She came back with a rocks glass of gin and tonic. "My favorite nightcap," she said, sipping it, then reclined against the headboard, stretching her legs. "When I was ten, I didn't know that Vietnam existed."

"When was that?"

"Nineteen sixty-eight."

"No kidding. Well, most Americans didn't know either."

"We all wore the buttons 'Part of the way with LBJ,'" she said. "Dad had one. He came home one day with a *Newsweek* with a cover picture of American GIs' bodies piled up on a tank during the Tet Offensive. He said, 'Goddamned war.'" She pulled up her leg and rested her glass on her knee. "How old were you then?"

"Twelve." I sat up, laced my hands in my lap to cover my nakedness. "I was nine when I saw the first American marines. They were on the ferry with us. They waved at us from their truck."

"Did they speak to you?"

"No, we just waved at each other. My mother told me to say hello. It sounded strange when I said it to them the first time. But they looked fascinating. Red-faced, rawboned, hairy. And big. They always smiled. In those early days they seemed to like children. Always tossed us chocolate bars, chewing gum sticks, and we would yell, *Americans number one*."

"We're the big brother to everyone. The world looks up to us."

"We did, too. I had classmates from poor families. Their parents sought work at the American base—Camp Evans, Camp Eagle. Hundreds of them waited outside the main gate every morning to be hired. A dollar a day. Menial jobs: they filled sandbags, picked up garbage, cut grass. Some dumped feces from the camp's latrines. The Americans called them 'shit burners.' But these people took their jobs seriously."

"Yuk. And they lived on such wages?"

"They subsist. But one dollar was decent money in Vietnamese piaster." I shook my head. "Even the children became garbage pickers. They haunted the garbage dump not far from the camp. They searched for unopened food cans and castoffs from GIs. My classmates brought them to the class to sell. Cans of peaches, meatloaf. We were fascinated. But they tasted strange. One day a kid in my class, one of the garbage pickers, came in with a patch on one of his eyes. He lost his eye."

"Got in a fight with some kids scavenging American food?"

"Explosives in the dump went off as he went through the trash. It'd happened before. The Americans set them there to scare off the garbage pickers."

"You sure? What the heck was it for?"

"Fun. They even tossed chocolate candy on the barbed wire and laughed when kids tore their flesh and their clothes trying to get to it."

"I still don't understand why—"

"American GIs became deadened by the war. They were pissed off at a lot of things. They were nice when they were first in country, but bad things happened to them. That was when the Americans stopped being nice to kids."

"They are human."

I knew she'd say that. "Another kid in my class didn't

show up for a week. You know what happened to him?"

Denise blinked.

"A US reconnaissance helicopter landed outside the city, and kids fought for C-ration cans the pilots threw at them. Then a pilot tossed out this can. My friend caught it, took a swig out of it as an elder screamed at him to stop. Guess what he drank? The helicopter hydraulic fluid. He became sick immediately, and they took him to an infirmary. He was forced to vomit until he passed out, but he remained sick for days."

Denise sipped a drink, her face impassive.

"Did you hate Americans?" she said. "You called them names?"

"Yes. *Mẽo.*"

"Gook." She gave me her glass after her retort. I sipped then placed the glass on her navel. She hit my hand. "Were you scared?"

"Of the Americans? I cheered for them when they seized the citadel from the VC. All it took was one gruesome month of communist occupation—I had had enough. My family lived inside the citadel."

"Where the king and queen used to live?" She took a quick sip. "I've read something about it."

"The Nguyen Dynasty. The royal family lived inside the Forbidden Purple City."

Denise's eyes opened wide. "Had you ever seen the king and queen?"

"That was before I was born."

Denise caressed the wall of her rocks glass. "Must be nice to live wealthy for the rest of your life on the king's money."

My eyes fell to the triangle patch below Denise's navel. She moved her rock glass down. I said, "Many historic structures were ruined during the Tet fighting. The Americans bombed the hell out of the citadel."

"Did they have a better choice?"

"Probably not. But they bombed the hell out of the civilian homes, too."

"All I know is our Marines kicked the VC's ass," Denise

said. "It was them who drove the Viet Cong out of the citadel, wasn't it?"

"A lot of people were killed, especially civilians."

"Like what happened at Mỹ Lai?"

"At Mỹ Lai the American soldiers murdered the Vietnamese civilians, but during Tet in Hue, the VC massacred the Vietnamese—their own people. Here you heard only of Mỹ Lai. The American public was more interested in a war crime committed by one American infantry platoon than in the Hue massacre."

I felt strange sitting naked next to her, looking at her nudity.

"I wasn't frightened, though," I said to her. "The adults were. My father wasn't home with us. The VC executed people like him. My mother kept the joss sticks burning on the altar every day and thanked the Buddha for sparing my father's life."

"Was your dad a big shot?

"No. He was a colonel."

"Why did the VC kill people like your dad?" Denise asked.

"Because he was classified as reactionary—anti-communist. The VC came into Hue with the names of those they wanted to kill. Few were spared. They executed government and military officials, political party officials, block leaders, intellectuals, teachers, even priests and monks. But they killed a lot of people out of personal hate and vendetta."

"Must've been hell . . . ."

"Every night we heard gunshots. Much later we found out that those were fired by the communists during their execution, and the playground of our high school was used as a mass grave." Now I felt cold on my torso, my nipples felt hard. "After the VC withdrew from Hue, folks came to dig for bodies. The odor from the rotten bodies hung for days over the neighborhood. Smelled like dead rats but with a fish stink. My mother burned incense in the house every day to kill that odor."

Denise tossed off her glass.

"We came back to our house inside the citadel," I said. "One side of the house had caved in. Must've been hit by artillery shells or helicopter gunships. Ammunition shells were all over the yard. You know what I saw on one side of our chest of drawers? An inscription: *Miami, FLA. Mom, Dad, and apple pie.* The American troops had boarded down in our house during the house-to-house combat against the VC."

"You were lucky. Old enough and you would've been shot by the VC bastards."

"They massacred at least a few thousand people. It took people months to search, to dig the mass graves. Mass graves in the schoolyards, in the parks of the inner city. Mass graves in the jungle creek beds, in the coastal salt flats. People shot to death, clubbed to death with pick handles, buried alive with elbows tied behind them. The communists said they executed only the reactionaries, those who worked for the South Vietnam government. But I saw many bodies of women and children. Shot in the head, bashed in the head. Did they deserve to die? I believe personal hate of one another . . . ."

Denise's head tilted to one side on the pillow, and she was breathing steadily. Her platinum hair shimmered in the reflection of the light. I took the rocks glass from her hand, pulled the quilt to her chest, and lay down beside her. I could smell the watermelon scent on her pillowcase. The room felt strange.

What I had told her about the massacre in Hue left an echo in my head. Fifteen years had passed. In this country, you don't see the gunships, the Skyraiders roaring every time you look up the sky. At night you don't hear the cannon booming in the distance, an AK-47 crackling down the street. The night flows into morning without curfew.

The summer before I left Vietnam for the United States under Uncle Vinh's sponsorship, a man came to our house. A prisoner just released from a reeducation camp, he said he knew my father. *The Colonel,* he said in a respectful tone. *How is he?* my mother asked timidly, as if fearing to hear the truth. No news is good news, they say. Every time I recalled that moment when the man told us about my father—the last time he saw him—I still felt a sudden flip in the pit of my stomach. My mother slumped to the rickety chair. She was fighting back tears so hard her face froze with a ghastly paleness. The image the man had created in my mind was demonic. I still saw it in my mind to this day. Three men huddled on the roadside in the rain. Held up by two cadres who wore pith helmets, the man in the middle had high cheek bones, the eyes seemed focusless like a blind man's eyes. The fierce ex-colonel. My father. He looked like a cadaver hoisted up to greet wayfarers. *What happened to him? What's wrong with him?* And the man said that was my father, last seen in Lao Cai, where he was being held. The Hanoi authorities moved the prisoners around after the '79 border war with China. *He looks dead*, the man said, using a milder word. He's lost the use of his legs. I heard my mother's cracked voice ask, *You mean he's a cripple?* The man nodded, avoiding my mother's eyes. *More or less. He's been kept in a CONEX container for the past two years. He had hepatitis, his eyesight was shot, and fungus grew on his skin. As long as he resists the system by refusing to sign his confession to his wrongdoings, he will remain there, losing more body parts.*

I knew that hate and revenge had a lot to do with the reeducation. When I left Vietnam, my father was still detained in a reform camp somewhere in the North.

After I settled in the United States, I had tried to adjust to its culture and adapt to its modern technology. I admired its democracy. But unlike many immigrants who tried to forget their past, I still carried with me the image of my country. That image was Hue, where my placenta was buried. Denise might never understand the nuances of the proverb I had told her. *Quê mẹ là nơi chôn nhau cắt rốn.* The Motherland is where we bury our placenta and sever our umbilical cord. It began with the cultural intellect of a city known for its moss-stained citadel, the imperial tombs nestled in the pine forest, temples and pagodas tucked away at the foot of gentle hills by a quiet stream. Its damp, foggy climate had left moisture damage on the age-old buildings, on houses with moss-covered *yin-yang* roof tiles. Through Hue flowed the Perfume River, clear and clean, and in the summer flame trees bloomed scarlet along its banks. All the streets were narrow, shaded with ancient trees, sometimes white with frangipani blossoms, sometimes pink with cassia. As a youngster, I lived in the Hue's mysterious atmosphere: half real, half magic. I used to walk home under the shade of the Indian almond trees, the poon trees. The nuts of the Indian almond trees tasted rich and fat like almonds, the nuts of the poon trees were polished and used in the marble games. At the base of these old trees, I would pass a shrine. If I went with my mother, she would push my head down. *Don't stare at it. That's disrespect to the genies,* my mother said.

It was the old capital of the Nguyen Dynasty. It was my birthplace.

The Devil's Mask

The stable boy peered up from the saddle when the little master made a grunt in his throat. Something was coming. Out in the sun, a white-furred monkey stood looking in. After a while, it waddled in and, once inside the dark stable, its fur looked as white as rice flour. It usually came when the little master was in the barn.

Now it sat crouched just like the little master, only smaller and wrinkle-faced like a prematurely aged child. The little master wore a little brass bell on a neck string; before he came hopping in—never walking like a normal person—the stable boy could tell who was coming. They always dressed him in a brightly colored outfit: this morning white shorts and a shirt in firecracker red. If he strayed from the house even after dark, the bright colors would help the servants find him. Now, he sat on the bed of cut hemp, watching the boy clean the saddle leather; he sniffed the oil the boy had just washed the leather with. The boy smoothed the saddle with a clean rag and watched him with wary eyes.

A noise at the door. The boy looked up. She was walking in; her boots made no sound on the thick hemp bedding. There you are, she said.

Ma'am, he said.

I thought this was where I would find him, she said with a cheerful smile as she glanced down at the little master, still half-crouched, next to the monkey. She stroked the monkey's balding head; it lifted its little face to her while scratching its cheek with its long hairy fingers. In the stall the stallion whinnied softly.

He knows you're here, the boy said, still holding the saddle in his hands. The saddle had the old leather smell and the oil smell from the polished brass buckles. I know, she said. What's wrong with my strap?

The horse'd been rubbing it against the fence post. It got ripped the other day.

She glanced down at the torn strap on the trestle table. Does it take long to fix that?

Not really.

I appreciate that, she said and brushed back the hair on her forehead. I have to take him in now for his medication.

What kind of medication?

Keeps him from being hyperactive.

He seems calm.

This monkey keeps him calm. She took the monkey's pink palm and laid it on the back of her hand. If he's here by himself, he'll likely make it hard for you to work.

I know. The boy hung his head to one side, eyeing the little master. How old is he now?

Fifteen.

He's a big-boned kid.

He can be as soft as a rabbit or out of control like a mad bull. I can't handle him as I used to. She took a deep breath. A faint smell hung in the high-ceilinged barn, this earthly smell of horse's sweat and hair, of leather and oil, of cut hemp and hay.

He could sense distress in her tone. You mean physically restraining him? he said.

She nodded. It takes two people now to hold him down. When that happens, I prefer men. She fell silent as she lay her eyes on him. He's awfully strong.

The boy drew imagined lines on the leather strap with the awl's tip. Will be harder when he gets older, he said. What'll happen then?

I've thought about that, she said as she reached down to stop the little master from grabbing the oil can on the table. I must have a plan. It was different when he was small. But I can't wish that on him. To stay small forever, even if I could.

What d'you mean?

He has to grow and mature. We all do. She smiled thinly, shaking her head at the little master. Then she made a sign to get his attention, and he rose to his feet. Standing, he was as tall as she; his long arms were big in the wrist, thick in the upper arm. He followed her out of the stable, hopping every three steps. The monkey hopped on all fours after him, and the little master, glancing back and shrieking, hopped away now from her and the monkey. When the monkey reached the gravel path that led down the slope, it stopped, sat back on its haunches, hands on the ground, and watched them going up to the veranda. After a while, it turned around and bounced across the grassy field toward the wooded hills beyond.

In the afternoon quiet blared a shrill voice from a loudspeaker mounted on the cab's top of a three-wheeled Lambretta as it made its way down the broken road that went around the foot of the hill. The patina-green Lambretta was weighed down with piles of household goods and an array of trappings. The voice called out, Anyone in need? Anything broke? Sell and fix right here on the spot, on the spot. The little three-wheeler chugged along, sounding out the announcement between short respites. Its clamor spooked the neighborhood dogs along the road, and suddenly they began to yelp and howl.

Sitting by himself at a dining table by the side French doors, the little master plugged his ears and howled. Soon, a maid came running out. Hush, she said. Hush now. The little master screwed his eyes shut, shaking his head in frenzy. His wailing got louder till the maid clamped his mouth with her hand, and he bit her. She slapped him on the side of the head, which set him bawling again, tears filming his burning eyes. Another maid, older than the first, hurried out from the interior. You keep quiet, you hear, keep it down, she said, stroking his back and pressing her cheek against his face. He banged his head against her face so hard she dropped to her knees. Devil you, she screamed. The shrill loudspeaker voice blasted again and again drew the dogs into a barking frenzy. Now the little master's body shook in fright, and he let out a mournful bawl. Helpless, the two women stood and watched, one rubbing her bitten finger, the other feeling her nose from the hit. From upstairs came a voice to chill them, shouting, Bring him up here!

The women started; they each tried to pull the little master up out of his chair, but he pushed them away. They closed back in, this time locking their arms under his. They lifted him. He kicked out his legs, knocking the cherry wood table sideways, and the glass of water and the box of medicine fell to the floor. The sound of broken glass froze the women. The master's hacking cough sounded right above them.

Go get Chung, the older maid said.

He's out in the field.

Get Ba.

The younger maid ran back into the dim corridor. Left alone, the older stood listening to the little master's bawling in the racket caused by the Lambretta's loudspeaker and the dogs. The hacking cough stopped; the voice again came down, Get him up here!

Yessir, the older woman glanced up at the presence from above. Ba will be here shortly. I'm terribly sorry, sir.

She walked around the little master in her bare feet, inspecting the shards of glass on the wood floor. A puddle of water had collected by a leg of the table. In the puddle, the box of medicine lay soaked. She bent close to the little master's tear-stained face. Stop now, she said. You don't want to go up there, or do you? She pulled back just as he flung out his arm, fist clenched, to hit her. She grappled with his arm; he spat at her. It hit her in the chest. Then, the outside racket had him cover his ears again. He bawled. The older maid was about to hush him with one hand over his mouth when the younger returned with a middle-aged man. Ba, the chauffeur, walked up to the little master, bent, and slipped his arms under the little master's. His hands locked he stood the little master up while the maids looked on. He dragged him to the staircase, up the steps, and the maids followed, each giving a push in the back. The wailing grew louder as the little master tried to free himself. He pulled back his head and spat in the chauffeur's face. The man quickly turned his face away, let the spit land on the side of his neck. The younger maid reached in with her hand and fastened the little master's mouth. On the landing the chauffeur paused, firmed his hold, and then stepped up the stairs. Bellowing, the little master lifted his face at the multi-tiered chandelier where sunlight coming through the high window sparkled in the crystal teardrops.

They reached the top step; when he saw the master sitting in the wheelchair in his white shirt and white trousers, the little master shot out his arm and grabbed the handrail's ornamental cap. Quickly the older maid peeled the fingers that grasped it. Huffing, the chauffeur dragged the manikin in his arms till he reached the wheelchair's footrest. As soon as he released him, the chauffeur grabbed the little master by the shoulders and pushed him down to his knees. The little master obliged, his wailing now just moans. As though they knew what to expect, the three servants stepped back, none leaving the scene, as the master wheeled the chair back just a few feet, reached down below the seat to lock the wheels. From his other hand, he pulled a stingray's tail whip, dried-out and black, its butt leather-wrapped. Outside the clamor was subsiding, the dogs whimpering now and then, the loudspeaker voice a distant echo.

The first lash caught the little master across the shoulder. His eyes opened wide, shocked by the pain. He raised himself up on his arms, letting out an inarticulate, angry cry. The second hitting his arm, he sank back down on his folded legs. He popped back up, shaking his head like a crazed animal, his face red, eyes feverish, and his sounds garbled. The whip cut the sound and caught him on an outstretched arm. He left that pleading posture and lunged to the wheelchair, grabbed the swing-out footrest, shaking it like he'd gone out of his mind, and, before the master could kick him, the chauffeur broke the hysterical critter's grip, forcing him, at the master's hand signal, face down on the floor. He had barely stepped out of the way when the whip cracked across the little master's back. It came down repeatedly. The little master shrieked defiance, banging his fists on the floor, trying to sit back up only to be pushed down by the chauffeur. Then the master gasped, stopped by a sudden cough. On the floor the little master whimpered, propping himself on his arms, his face tearstained.

At the master's wave of dismissal, the servants each grabbed a limb of the little master as they stood him on his feet. His shorts were wet on the front, and urine was running down the sides of his legs. He never stopped whimpering while the chauffeur dragged him back downstairs. The two maids flanked them going down the steps like taking back an inmate.

The master came out of his nap and saw her lift the birdcage from the veranda's railing. She pushed his chair back into the coolness of their bedroom and parked his chair so he could sit looking out over the white railing to the horizon, now blushing a rose hue. The birdcage in hand, she went out to the hallway, and, when she came back, empty handed, she locked the bedroom door, picked up a bottle of baby oil, and knelt down in front of the wheelchair's footrest.

I saw that you already fed him, she said, placing the bottle on the floor, and pulled down his trousers by the waistband.

Yes. He was calling for you to feed him. The master pushed himself up slightly, so she could slip his trousers past his buttocks. She was his second wife, after his first wife—mother of his idiot son—died from cancer.

She touched the felt heat pad that covered his pubes and genitals. The heat had mostly gone from it. Hold it, she said, and placed the pad in his lap. The skin of his pubis felt warm against her palm. His penis felt warm too, resting limp and curved like a crooked finger. She squeezed a few drops of oil into her palm, lemon fragrant and cool, smoothed the length of his penis with her palm. Circling her thumb and forefinger round the base of it, she began to push her fingers upward the shaft, to the glans. She stopped, holding the grip momentarily, returned her fingers to the base of the penis and started over. The heat from the pad had made the flesh firm, the skin soft and oiled, so she did not have to labor with her gripping stroke.

A raspy cough came from the hallway. It sounded like his cough. Sometimes it confused her to think that he was awake, for the mynah was the incarnation of every animate soul whose voice or sound had ever come to its hearing. She liked to listen to its clear, ringing voice that carried far when it whistled. But it stopped its whistling habit so it could mimic human voices, except when it began to mimic the cat, it grated on her nerves. Once it could talk, it never ceased. At night she hung the cage in the corridor and covered it with a black cloth so it wouldn't be tempted. One night while she was taking a bath, the bedroom door closed, a maid came up with her husband's herbal medicine and knocked. Before she could get out of the bathroom, she heard the bird out in the hallway repeating, Open the door, open the door.

The master's hand now came to rest on her shoulder, squeezing it through the soft cotton bathrobe still damp with her body's wetness. His cheeks hollowed as he sucked in his breath while stroking the side of her neck, his fingers dry. Yet the fever in him never made a difference, even with her patient strokes, long and gripping, to force blood into the organ, which had been a daily routine, once in the early morning and again before bedtime, lasting each time fifteen minutes. Not even a maid was allowed to know, much less to perform the exercise in her absence as a chore to cure his dysfunction.

❖

At sunset the chauffeured car brought her back from the town. Behind the hill the sunset reddened the sky, and the lighthouse, ocher yellow and pencil thin, peeked above the dip of the hill.

Surrounding the bungalow where servants, maids, and the stable boy stayed were sea almond trees, old, vase-shaped crowns dense and dark with leathery broad leaves now losing their last luster in the evening dark. Someday, she thought, she'd learn how to paint, and the first thing she'd paint was the autumnal leaf colors of sea almond. Copper, red, yellow. The maroon of the fruit. The dark red of the leaves, before they all fell.

It was quiet in the house. She looked at herself in the wall mirror. Her mirror image in the black-and-white plaid skirt behind the flower vase. In the vase the water smelled fresh. The maid must have changed it in the afternoon, she thought. One dining table's end chair was not pushed in like the rest; it was turned out to the alcove, which was lit dimly with its recessed light. In a glimpse, she thought the chair was a photograph with its muted honey-colored satinwood, its curved legs flowing gracefully. She walked across the bamboo floor, hearing only the sound of her heels, stopping near the chair to pick up a bird feather, fluffy and purplish black. She set the chair back in its usual solemn position, wondering how the mynah's feather had gotten here. By the alcove, she held the feather under the recessed light. It was indeed the mynah's. Standing alone in the alcove was a Kangxi antique china vase. Ancient, permanent, defying time.

As she mounted the stair steps, she remarked the unusual quiet in the house. Halfway up, she expected the mynah to greet her, *Hello Ly.* But she heard nothing. The bird cage wasn't in the hallway at its normal spot. Her husband must have taken it with him to the veranda, she thought.

Coming through their bedroom, she saw him out on the veranda, in his wheelchair, his back toward her. There was no bird cage with him that she could see. She closed the screen door behind her. The wind was warm, rustling the leaves, dark and glittering with fireflies. The sea cadenced with the sound of waves. His white shirt and the white railing shimmered. He didn't look up at her as she came to his side.

Who took the birdcage? she said, looking down at him.

There isn't one anymore, he said, still not looking at her.

What happened?

He took it downstairs. Played with it. Made the bird call out to the cat. That vicious cat you allowed him to keep in his room. When the cat came, he opened the cage door.

She remembered the mynah's feather.

The cat chewed the bird, he said, paused by a sudden cough.

She could imagine flesh and bones and feathers while the little master watched and made those crazy sounds.

I could hear him from up here, the master said. Then I heard the maids and knew.

She felt nauseated. She didn't want to ask what came after the incident. Instead, she turned and went back in, closing the screen door. Downstairs, through the colonnaded archway, she went the length of the unlit corridor to the kitchen, brightly lit, and the air moist and rich with cooking smells. The older maid stood by the stove, her apron's string tied across her broad back, ladling soup from a stainless steel pot into a crock. At the kitchen table sat the younger maid, her left arm in a sling. The young maid, hearing her footsteps, looked up.

Good evening, ma'am, the maid said.

Good evening, she said, nodding at both of them just as the older maid turned around from the stove.

Dinner will be ready shortly, ma'am, the older maid said, resting the wooden ladle against the pot's handle.

I'm not checking on that, she said, stepping past the doorless entrance into the ceramic-tiled kitchen. What I want to know is how he went upstairs and took the birdcage without any of you knowing it?

The maids dropped their gaze. She waited. Then the older maid said, I was bringing lunch out to the field for my husband. He was busy by himself 'cos a cow was having a calf. I should've taken the little master along with me. She paused, her fingers playing with the hem of her apron. I'm very sorry for what happened, ma'am.

She thought, then said to the younger maid, What about you? Where were you then when she was out?

The younger maid gulped. I was with him, ma'am. I gave him the medicine. He fell asleep after that, so I went to take a shower. I didn't know he woke out of it. It never happened before, and I knew how long he'd sleep 'cos of those pills. When I heard him bawling, I ran into the dining room, and there he was with the bird and the cat. It was such a mess.

She watched the young servant crying, said nothing. After a while she said, What happened to your arm?

I pulled him up, told him to be quiet. The maid shook her head. I just couldn't move him at all. Couldn't quiet him, either. Then, I tried to yank him up, and he got upset and grabbed my arm and twisted it bad. It hurt so much I screamed, and then I heard the master from upstairs to tell him to quiet, and I ran outside to get Ba. He was sleeping when I woke him. But Ba couldn't drag him nowhere this time, so I ran out and found Mr. Qui. He was busy tending the garden, but he came in, and he and Ba finally got him up off the floor and took him upstairs. He was punished, and I couldn't dare look. Then the master told us to take him back down to his room.

Is that all? she asked.

The maid said nothing, her eyes to the floor. Then she shook her head. No, ma'am.

What else? she asked.

The master gave an order, and Ba did what he was told.

She kept silent, waiting, yet her stomach churned.

The maid wiped her nose with the back of her hand. Ba found the cat somewhere in the house and took it outside. Ma'am, you'll have to ask him where he buried the cat.

She felt disoriented. Then the turbulence passed. How badly are you hurt? she said calmly.

The doctor told me I had a sprained elbow, the younger

maid said. It hurt bad when it popped, but now it's not hurting as bad.

She looked at both of them, and they both bent their heads down. What about him? she said. Has he been looked after?

Yes, ma'am, the younger said, peering up.

Has he been let out?

No, ma'am.

It's dinner time. Well, let me make sure he behaves. I don't want hell in this house.

She turned to leave. The younger maid called out, He's not allowed any visit.

I'll make the rule for you. With that said, she walked down the corridor and went around the staircase, entered the other archway and down the hallway to where his room was, the last of the several rooms reserved for guests. She turned the doorknob. Locked. It was an oak door, thicker than ordinary, to deaden the bawls he would make. It could be locked only from the outside. She got the key from the hallway sideboard and opened the door. It felt heavy to open.

There was no light in the room. She reached for the wall light switch and flipped it on. The single ceiling lamp shone a soft amber. The room, having a bed, a dresser, no wall mirrors, was thickly carpeted—the only room in the house so. There was no table lamp, for he had played with the light bulbs and crushed them with his hands. The bed sat low, its curved legs sturdy looking. He sat on the floor at the footboard, both hands tied to the leg of the bed. She saw that he wore a black mask, the devil's mask worn by the hamlet's lobster hunters. The mask, fashioned after the devil's pod of water caltrop in glossy black, was sculpted to resemble a leering goat-horned demon. Seeing him tied up with such a mask on, as if he was being sacrificed to some dark gods, she held her breath momentarily, then sat down by him. He could see her through the eye slits, because he dropped his head in submission. She stared at red welts, now masked by ointment, on the back of his neck. She could see them on his arms, and, as she stroked his thick back, running her hand softly over his shirt, she didn't want to look under it. After a while, she tilted the mask up on his face and worked it back to free it from the strap. Across his cheek lay a purplish gash.

She held his head in her arms. He glanced up at her, fevered eyes watery.

The Girl on the Bridge

Before sunset, through my window, the wild red banana flowers glint golden on their pointed tips.

I was seventeen when I saw from a bridge that savage red among the green of banana fronds. It was an early Sunday afternoon, and I was coming home with my Chinese friend, Huan, from a peasant's house where we students took up residence during the week. We had moved with our school out of the city after the Americans began bombing North Vietnam. On this morning, we had heard the air raid sirens, and we were biking toward the bridge into the city before the planes showed up. We were on the bridge just as the American jets came roaring over. I had barely jumped off my bicycle when the explosions blasted the air with a furnace heat. The river gushed up as a bomb hit the water, then the bridge shook and clanged. Dirt stung my eyes, my nose. The air singed. Stinging hot on the skin. Suffocating me with its burned-match odor.

I was lying on my back on the bridge. Pain shot up to my head. I found myself away from the wreckage of the bridge. Metal scraps, bent and twisted, were littered on the deck. An iron top brace from the bridge, completely torn off, had trapped both of my legs. The pain throbbed in my temples. With my arm flung over my face, I saw a blue sky. Dust fell into my eyes. I turned my head sideways and saw the railroad track gleaming down the center of the bridge and metal debris strewn everywhere.

"Giang!" My friend Huan began pulling at my arm.

I heard shouts, footfalls. I shook my head at Huan. His face, smeared with dust, looked like a stranger's face. People were running up from the other end of the bridge that led into the city. They wore dark-colored pantaloons, black trousers. Like a horde of giants about to trample me. They all wore pith helmets. They stared down at me, and someone touched the heavy iron bracing that trapped my legs. "How're your legs?" he asked, bending over me. "Can you feel anything in your legs?" Another man peered into the dark crevice under the iron beam. "How do we get him out of this?" the first man said. I looked up at Huan, his face drawn up painfully. Suddenly, I heard more planes. "Comrades!" a man shouted. "Take cover!" They all dove to the floor of the bridge, and Huan collapsed on top of me, his hands covering his head. The planes swooped down low, so close that I could see the pilots' heads in the cockpits. The planes fired at the bridge, and the gun muzzles flashed in the sun, the throaty bursts of guns steady, the shrieking noises of metal against metal when volleys hit the bridge. I wrapped my head with my arms and forgot the pain in my legs. The ground shook. Bursts of gunfire came up from the ground at the other end of the bridge: the machine guns, the antiaircraft battery. Wind-borne smoke, thick and pungent, drifted across the bridge. Soon the guns died down, the planes droned away, and the air was tinged with a hot-metal smell. My friend rose, dusted his hair with his hands. "Can you feel your legs, Giang?" he asked. I nodded, licking away gritty dirt on my lips. "How bad?" he asked, clasping my hand. "It hurts," I said. His soft hands pressed hard against my hand. People were yelling from the bridge's end, where the gun emplacements were dug in, well-camouflaged with green-leafed branches. They came running onto the bridge, joining those who had showed up earlier. Two men, wearing goggles, appeared to be the gunners, and a girl in a white short-sleeved shirt and black trousers carried a first aid bag over her shoulder.

The taller man pushed up his goggles to the crown of his head and looked me over. "Gotta send for help," he said. "We can't do a thing here for the boy."

The man in the pith helmet, who had wondered how to

remove me from the wreckage, raised his voice: "We can't cut through the iron with bare hands."

The taller man singled out a man who had high, sharp cheekbones. "Go to the city. Get those who can do the job out here. Hurry!"

"Yes, comrade," said the chosen man. "The city got bombed too. Don't know if they will send anyone our way."

"Tell 'em we've got no equipment here. They'll understand."

"Yes, comrade."

The tall man looked at the girl, then back down at me. "She'll take care of you. We have to use runners now for things like this. Our telephone lines are down."

I nodded. He had a solemn face like one of my schoolteacher's. A face I could trust. His olive-green khaki shirt had sweat stains on the armpits. After he ordered his men to their tasks, he knelt beside me, across from Huan. "You must be brave," he said to me.

"Yes, sir." I felt drained from fighting the pain.

He looked at Huan. "Are you with him?"

"Yes," Huan said meekly. "He's my friend."

"Stay with him or go tell his parents."

"Yes, sir."

The man studied my face. I fought back the pain, trying to look calm. I felt sweat break out on my forehead. The man, pushing on his knee to rise, said to me, "I have to leave you here. Is there anything else you want to ask me?"

I hadn't asked him anything yet, but I shook my head. "Can I have a cigarette?"

He sat back down, his shoulders drawn up. "You need a cigarette? Ah. The pain must be very bad then." He went into his shirt front pocket and placed a cigarette pack in my hand. "Keep it, son. It'll be a while."

He dug into his trousers pocket, fished out a matchbox, and placed it in my hand. I said, "Thank you, sir," as he left. I grabbed Huan's arm. "Go home. It's not safe here."

"What about you? You're not safe here, either."

I raised myself up on my elbow. "If I could walk like you—" I stopped. Pain seized me.

The girl swung her bag down. It had a red cross painted inside a white circle on its front. "How's your pain?" she asked gently, flinging back her long hair plait over her shoulder.

"It's there," I said. "Can you spare me a sip of water?"

She handed me the bottle and waited as I tipped it. Her large eyes watched me calmly. When I handed her the bottle back, my hand touched hers. Something tender permeated my soul. I kept myself propped up on my elbow. I didn't want to lie down while she cleaned my face. I held still. A sudden stab of pain in my legs jerked my body uncontrollably.

"You must be hurting badly," she said as she poured water from a bottle onto a white kerchief. "Let me wash your face."

"Do you have aspirin for him?" Huan asked.

"Yes," she said. She searched through the bag. "I was about to give him some."

She let me hold the bottle and fed two pills into my mouth. They tasted sour.

"That should keep the pain at bay for a while," she said, folding the kerchief.

"How soon can they be here?" Huan pulled at her elbow.

"It'll be a while," I said. "Go home. There's nothing you can do here."

"But I can't leave you here," he said, almost pleading with me.

"I'll keep an eye on him," she said. "Because I don't know when help will arrive."

"Go!" I raised my voice. "Your parents might try to find you."

He rose to his feet and stood looking around. "What about your bicycle?"

"Leave it there," I said.

"Do you want to read in the meantime? I'll leave you a novel. You want it or not?"

The pain flared. "Read a novel?" I snapped at him. "With this pain—"

"Do you want me to read it to you?" she said.

I nodded, then shook my head. The pain clouded my thinking. But I would not let her treat me like a person on his deathbed. My friend waved at me as he walked to his bicycle. I watched him tottering to find his balance on the wheels until he rode off. I should have kept my temper with him. I dropped my gaze. The nurse's sandaled feet were next to my elbow. Plain toenails, neatly clipped.

"Where do you live?" she asked softly.

I caught my breath and told her where I stayed in the city.

"Your parents might worry themselves sick," she said.

"I live with my friend's family."

"Are you from the city? Born here?"

Again, I nodded. Her large eyes held a gentle look.

"You don't speak with the city accent," she said.

"No, actually I'm not from here. Where I'm from . . . ." I tried to shift my weight to ease the pain numbing my leg. ". . . it's in the countryside, an hour from here by train."

"So, your parents have no way of knowing . . . ."

I shifted my body to ease the numbness on my arm and lit a cigarette.

"Do you want to rest your head?" she asked.

"Rest my head?"

"Yes. Here," she said, placing the first-aid bag behind me. "Lie back and rest."

I did what she told me, the cigarette in my mouth, my face upturned looking at her long plait hanging down her front, black against her white shirt.

"How old are you?" she asked.

"Seventeen." I took another drag. The nicotine helped relieve the pain. "What about you?"

"Eighteen." She glanced at my cigarette as I tapped it with my finger to break the ash. "You smoke often?"

I nodded.

"Since when?"

"Fifteen."

"Fifteen?" She arched her brows. "Why?"

"It kept me warm. Those cold mornings when I had on just a shirt. I sat in a market and wrote letters for those who couldn't read or write."

"You were a scribe?"

"Something like that." I swallowed the smoke. "If they wanted to make out an application or petition, or needed to write a letter to someone, they would tell me their stories. I put them down in words. It was so cold some mornings my hand shook. I couldn't hold the pen. A man let me have a puff of his hand-rolled cigarette and said, 'Keep ye warm, eh?' It surely did. I smoked their cigarettes till I had enough money to buy our northern cigarettes."

"Your parents didn't reprimand you for smoking?"

I inhaled the smoke deeply, held it until the pain dimmed. The sun was behind her, bronzing the railings of the bridge, and the contour of her head glowed golden. I pinched a shred of tobacco from my lip. "My father just let me take care of myself. I was old enough."

"At fifteen?"

"He wasn't around anymore when I was fifteen."

"What about your mother?"

"She died when I was five. Then, when I was twelve my father died. So, I left my village and went to the city and stayed with my friend's family. We used to go to our village school together before the Land Reform in the North." I took one last drag, drawing hard, until the cigarette burned to my thumb and finger, and I flicked it away. The men in pith helmets were directing traffic on the bridge—cyclists, pushcarts, light trucks—routing them to the other side of the track, leaving it empty on my side. They tossed metal bits onto wheelbarrows, and the metal clanged noisily, and soon they carted off the rubble in wheelbarrows one after another, rolling on their squeaky rubber wheels into the slanting saffron-yellow beams of sunlight. "I used to be my father's helper after school when I was eight. Learned how to haggle for every xu we earned from selling stuff."

She rested her chin in her hands. "What stuff?"

I did not look at her but at the rusty red on the collapsed brace that weighed on my lower legs. I tapped out another cigarette and saw her eyes fall to the cigarette. I waved the match out, holding the smoke in my mouth as long as I could, and drove the smoke out of my nostrils. "My father," I said, meeting her gaze, "caught snakes for a living. Eventually he died from a snakebite. Before that he was one of the wealthy landowners in the southern region of the Red River Delta."

She nodded. "Land Reform changed many people's fortunes. But I've never met anyone in real life who was a victim of the purge. At least until now."

"Those people died from execution. If they survived that, they'd later die from hunger. They weren't allowed to work a decent job unless they left their native place." I cupped the cigarette against my lips so she couldn't see me swallowing the smoke. It numbed my head, took my mind off my legs. I spoke through my clenched fist. "In the beginning, my father broke rocks. He owned a hammer and anvil, nothing else—except for his moon lute. He broke rocks and sold the chips to those who needed them for road and housing construction. Sold them or traded them for food: manioc, rice vermicelli, salted duck eggs. Broke rocks from dawn to dusk. I helped. I was eight years old then. He got me a smaller hammer, taught me how to pound rocks without hurting my wrist, how to whack them without blinding my eyes with flying chips. Broke rocks, both of us. Till one day his back gave out. Then he started catching snakes. Breaking rocks you sit in one place all day long. But catching snakes you must go from place to place. By evening, your legs are dead. He got a large jar of *tam xà* liquor, his only treasure besides his moon lute, and he rubbed his legs at night with the snake liquor."

"What's the *tam xà* liquor?" she asked.

"You catch three kinds of snakes and then preserve them whole in a jar of liquor. The *tam xà* make up that special liquor." I coughed and told her what I remembered vividly, that through that clear jar you could see the snakes coil up in it, one on top of another in their beautiful colored spots.

"Heavens!" she blurted. "Three kinds of snakes? Dead?"

"Yeah. The spectacled cobra, the banded krait, and the rat snake." I drew deeply on my cigarette. "After he killed them, he would hold each of them up by the head and squeeze its body down the length to the tail until a green slime oozed from its anus. He said if you don't do that, the snake liquor will stink."

She shook her head.

"He smoked hand-rolled cigarettes," I said, "and drank snake liquor every night till he passed out. Played his moon lute in our early days after we'd lost everything. The lute was the only thing left with him, kept him company at night when he played. Then he started getting drunk every night, and I had to wrap the lute and put it away. He didn't want to look at it anymore because it reminded him of his wealthy past. He kept going because of me. Without me, he was better off dead. I knew that."

"I thought they killed all the landlords during the Land Reform."

"The People's Court did that to most of them, those condemned by the peasants, the wretched poor, the labors-for-hire. If you were rich and cruel to the poor, you were doomed even before the People's Court handed down the verdict. Most of them got buried alive because the firing squad couldn't shoot them dead—they never fired a gun before. But if you were rich and your cruelty wasn't notorious, you'd get sent to prison. And if you were rich and not cruel to the poor, you'd only lose all your wealth and get the first taste of how to be dirt poor. That was my father's fate."

"Where were you when all this was happening to your father?"

"I was in the crowd watching him suffer humiliation."

"By whom?"

"Those who worked for our family. Now they turned against him. They accused him of all things imagined. Many of these folks couldn't read and write, so the Viet Minh cadres would put them through rehearsals before the denunciation sessions. The cadres taught them the hand gestures, made them memorize words and phrases so it would look real and spontaneous. I watched my father crawl on his hands and knees to the dirt platform before the tribune. Fourteen of them, all illiterate peasants, sat on the lowest tier and seven more on the middle tier, and there were huge pictures of Mao Tse-Tung and Ho Chi Minh on the top tier. His former employees took turns to denounce him with insults and accusations. The committee chief, a woman on the middle tier, would shout down at him, commanding him to rise and fall on his knees again and again. My father lasted the early part of the day before he was dragged to the tribune to sign his confession. He confessed to everything he was accused of. Many of the accusations were make-believe. The most wicked landowners would suffer the trial for two or three days before they were executed."

She cupped her face and peered down at me through the gaps between her fingers. "They took everything away from him after that?"

"Yeah."

"So where was home after that?"

"In a graveyard. He fixed up a shelter, and we stayed there, and soon I found all kinds of snakes also living there. The graveyard soil was peat soil, and during the rainy season the top layer would drift, and what grew on it were sedges and peat moss and reed grass, which attracted the cuckoos to build their nests there. Soon I found out that cuckoos fed on snakes. They would pound the snakes to death with their strong bills and swallow them headfirst. We got used to living with birds and snakes. We knew about snakes like we knew about the weather. So, when my father quit breaking rocks, he knew what to do next."

"But how do you make a living catching snakes?"

"You sell snake meat to the eateries and the gallbladders to the Chinese herbal stores."

"I could imagine eating birds in any imaginable way." She shook her head. "But not snakes."

"Snake meat is tasty. You can't tell if it's chicken or fish—if you don't know what you're eating. But the snake's gallbladder is what medicine men like those Chinese herbalists wanted most."

"Gallbladder? Why would they want that?"

"He said different parts of a snake have different medicinal values. Said if you sun-dry a snake body and then cut it up and grind the pieces into powder, then you can cure stomach and intestinal problems because it's high in protein and enzymes. But the *tam xà* gallbladders brought him more money from the Chinese men than anything he could make off a snake without its gallbladder."

"Why those three kinds?"

"They're poisonous snakes. My father hunted just those three kinds. After he got a basket full of them, he'd bring them to the herbal stores. He laid down the basket on the floor and began chewing a wad of wild tobacco he used to roll cigarettes with. Then he rubbed his hand and forearm with the chewed tobacco and opened the basket's lid and snatched up a spectacled cobra. He got the cobra by the neck with one hand and squeezed it so hard its mouth flew open wide and you could see its long ugly fangs. Behind the counter the Chinese owner folded his arms and watched as my father drove a small, pointed knife into the midsection of the cobra and slit it open. In no time he gouged out a blue-black thing like an egg. He plopped it down on a saucer and tossed the dead snake back into the basket. The dead snakes would later end up in the eateries. Brought him much less than gallbladders. Then he grabbed a banded krait. Beautiful snake with black and yellow bands. This type has a blue-green gallbladder. Then he got the rat snake, the smallest of the three."

"But what kind of medicinal value do these snake gallbladders have?"

"For treatment of bronchitis and cough." I waved off the cigarette smoke that made her squint. "They heat-dry the gallbladders and grind them with dried tangerine peels to powder. It's one of the best cough medicines."

She laced her hands in her laps, watching me draw my last drag. "Someday you'll need that cough medicine yourself. My uncle is a heavy smoker. Whenever I hear the sound of coughing, I know it's him."

Her tone soothed me. I cupped the cigarette with my other hand and spat out shreds of tobacco on my tongue. "My friend Huan said the same thing. His father is a Chinese herbalist, lives a healthy life, so I respect that. At night when I need a puff of cigarette, I go outside on the street."

"Has his father ever bought snake gallbladders from snake catchers?"

I couldn't help grinning. She smiled.

"He has," I said. "Sometimes they bring him one of those three kinds because they know what he wants. These weren't snake catchers by trade, though. So, none of them knew how to remove a snake's gallbladder. I would slit the snake open and take out its gallbladder for him."

The noises of the wheelbarrows grew fainter beyond the bridge. A breeze came up, fanning my face. In a brief lull, I heard my stomach grumbling. She asked me to sit up and reached for her bag. She went through it, and her hand came out holding a small bundle of brown paper. She slid the bag back under me.

"You're hungry, right?" Inside the paper was a smaller bundle wrapped in a banana leaf.

I was starving. I had not eaten since we left the peasant's house in the morning. She peeled away the banana-leaf wrapping. I could smell the fresh leaf as she gave me a rice dumpling.

She brought the other dumpling to her lips and took a small bite. Inside the white glutinous dumpling was a red bean paste. It tasted mildly sweet.

"Where'd you get them?" I asked.

"I made them. They're my lunch."

I stopped eating. "Now you'll go half hungry."

She smiled. "I wish we had mushroom and pork cubes to make the fillings. Tastier. We can buy fish only once a month.

Rarely meat."

"Do you have a big family?"

"Five of us and my parents."

"What's your father do?"

"He works at a factory. My mother and I wake up at five in the morning, so she can cook breakfast and lunch for Father to take with him to work. The same for breakfast and lunch every day: cooked vegetables and rice. Sometimes she packs a steam-cooked manioc and sprinkles brown sugar on it. That's dessert for him. We have government food ration. For all city people. We might get chicken once every three months. And since we can afford fish only once a month, it's a treat. I don't remember what pork or chicken tastes like anymore."

I sighed. The last bite of dumpling seemed stuck in my throat. She saw me try to sit up and quickly got out the bottle of water.

"Take a big gulp," she said.

I washed it down and handed her back the bottle. She still had half the dumpling between her fingers. I had drunk her water and eaten her food. She'd hardly sipped her water. I knew how it felt living on food ration. Your life was continually preoccupied with food. Looking at her holding half the dumpling in one hand, the bottle of water in the other, I felt very tender toward her. I told her in the city quarter where I stayed, there was a public water tap on each street. I always drank from the tap, never bottled water like her. She said she never drank tap water but would carry it home in a five-gallon pail. She had to make several trips, standing in a long line each time, to fetch enough water for the whole family to cook, bathe, drink. For drinking water, she boiled tap water and bottled it so her father could make tea when he got home from work. By the time he came home, her mother had already gone to the city stores to buy food and household items. Rice, firewood for cooking and heating were the most expensive.

"What're you doing out here on a Sunday?" I asked as she eased the last bit of dumpling into her mouth.

"I'm a volunteer in the City Vanguard Youth," she said, covering her mouth with her hand.

"Some of the boys I know volunteer, too. They said if you volunteer, the government will exempt you from the military service. Said if you're classified as sons or daughters from a bourgeois or landlord class, the government will erase it from the record."

"Why didn't you volunteer, then?" she asked as she folded the banana leaf.

"They can erase my bad classification all they want, but that won't make it right for me and my father."

"But you can join the Vanguard Youth to help clean up the city, help the wounded after we're bombed by the Americans." She said she belonged to a platoon that was stationed at this bridge. Her platoon was part of a company which made up a battalion that employed the city youths like her to repair roads and build pontoon bridges where main bridges got bombed.

I dropped my gaze to her hands. She was wrapping the folded banana leaf inside the brown paper and folding them up together. She saw me watching and said, "I reuse them. Sometimes we can't even buy banana leaves."

The sun was low now on the horizon where the river glinted red. Shadows grew across the bridge spreading to the riverbank, which was thick and green with banana groves. In the deep green of banana fronds were splashes of red flowers.

"Aren't they beautiful?" she asked, following my gaze.

I nodded, enthralled by the banana flowers' breathtaking, cardinal red. There was a racket on the bridge, and we both turned to look. A railroad trolley was coming toward us. One man was pushing it, and three others were running alongside the track.

"Here they come," she said. "They'll have the equipment to cut the metal for you."

Suddenly I felt hollow. I didn't feel relieved as the men arrived. She stood up, looked down at me, her plait falling across her chest. Her face was shadowy in the twilight,

and on the riverbank the last glimmer of sun glowed golden
on the pointed tips of wild banana flowers.

Night, This River

1

They came to a river town. After she brought the boat to a dock, she went up the cement steps onto a narrow street and into a shop shaded by a yellow awning. He stood up in the boat, looking across the waterfront where row after row of merchant boats were moored to the end of the street of the floating market, where townspeople stood leaning down from the concrete railings, haggling over the prices of fish, fruits, vegetables; buying foods wrapped in banana leaves, in bowls smoking with steam, in multi-decked tin containers they brought to take foods home. Poling oars at rest crisscrossed one another, soaring from the water in pale blue ripples as blue as cooking smoke, thinly drifting, that palled the river.

He sat down on the tackle box, closed his eyes against the sun, chin tucked against his chest, and sleep came easily.

The shaking of the boat woke him.

Are you hungry, Nam? she said to him, standing with the sun behind her back. He looked at a small paper bag in her hand. *That can't be a meal.*

I'll eat when you eat, he said.

You're sweet. Come, meet my husband.

He entered the compartment, his legs bent in the low, curving dome. A stench hit him. It stopped him on his feet. The long, roofed compartment was sectioned off by another curtained door. On a wooden-plank floor lay a man facedown, clad in a black, short-sleeved shirt. Flies buzzed over him.

Damn flies again, the woman said and grabbed a straw hand fan and started fanning back and forth.

He let out his breath. Why not put up a mosquito net for him, he said.

My husband said it made him feel like he's dying.

The man turned his head toward them. It didn't look like he was sleeping. His hair was closely cropped, his bushy eyebrows met above his eyes. You got the medicine? he asked the woman. A deep scar ran across his lower lip to his chin.

The woman nodded. She brought a pail filled with water and came to kneel by the plank bed. The boy sat down on his haunches alongside the woman, noticing that the man didn't even look at him.

Raise up, the woman said.

As the man humped his back, the woman removed his shirt. It took all but a second for the boy to smell an oppressive odor that rose from the man's back. Boils. Walnut-sized boils leaking pus in yellowish green. The inside of his shirt was stained with off-colored blotches.

He watched the woman trying to squeeze a pus-filled boil with her thumbs. She strained herself, leaning down with her weight. It didn't tear. Then the man reached under the pillow and pulled out an oyster knife, shaking it in the air.

Use this, he said. And then at her hesitancy he snapped. Do it, for fuck's sake.

She brought the knife's pointed tip against the boil's head. It'll hurt, she said.

They been hurting like hell all night long, he said. I didn't sleep a damn wink.

She pushed in the knife's tip and pressed down with her other thumb. It squirted pus and hit her between the eyes. She flinched. Yellow pus tinged with blood. She laid the knife on his back and wiped her face with her hand. The man grunted. She picked up the knife again and gashed another boil. A while later, pus and blood streaked freely down his back, running off his sides onto the planks. The flies came alighting on the pus-smeared boils, and some of them sat on his back, drinking the yellow fluid. The boy could smell the bad odor now. Perhaps lying prone was the only way to sleep, he thought.

From the paper bag the woman picked up a bottle of alcohol, wet a small piece of cloth with it, and began wiping the man's back till it was just raw-looking with reddish lumps. He didn't even recoil. She pinched some white powder and sprinkled it on the erupted boils. The stink tinged with alcohol hung wetly in the air. As she rinsed and washed the cloth, the flies circled the soiled shirt.

Get me some liquor, the man spoke into his pillow.

She handed him a square-looking bottle. He uncorked it quickly and took a long swig from it. Then he snorted and buried his face in the pillow. The woman pinched the shirt from the floor and dropped it into the pail, where it sank slowly into the brownish water.

I've just got us a boy here, the woman said to the man. He'll help us till you get well again.

Help with what? the man said, his voice muffled.

Fishing. What else?

Bottom net-fishing you mean?

Exactly what I mean.

Take him to Black Carp Run early tomorrow. One-day trial. Or I'll have to split my fucking self in half to do it.

You don't have to be rude to him, the woman said gently. Can you?

I wouldn't fucking know. If these boils don't leave me alone soon, and if you keep picking up shitbrains along the way like you did before, we won't have a boat to fish comes tomorrow when the goddamn banker shows up.

What else did you want me to do that I haven't done? Maybe the next time you can be the talent judge, since you're a real fisherman.

Shut the fuck up! He raised himself up and then slumped back down.

The boy looked at the man's bare, muscular torso, copper-brown and lean, and was taken in by the tattoo sleeves of huge water serpents intricately done in red-blue hues. He felt pity for the woman, but he held no ill feeling toward the man.

Sir, he said in a low voice to the man, I can bottom-fish for you.

When I see it, the man said without looking at him, I'll believe it.

Yessir.

I want that cargo deck filled with fish again. I want to hear them jump and smack their fucking lives out in there. Day and night. That's money to my ear. Got me?

I got you, sir.

Listen boy . . . .

His name is Nam, the woman said.

Tell me the size of your net, the man said.

Seventeen feet long, eight feet deep, sir.

Ever used ten feet deep?

No, sir.

Why not?

My uncle, he didn't like it. Said it's too long and fish could get out under the edge of the footrope.

Your uncle? Then why're you here?

Before he died, sir.

The man said nothing, then he raised his head from the pillow, tilted the bottle, and sucked from it with a pop. How many meshes you got on the eight feet deep? he said and burped.

About hundred and ten. Three inches in their mesh opening, sir.

And the lead?

The lead weight? One every five mesh openings on the footrope. Same with the floats on the headrope.

The man said nothing. He seemed to be thinking, but the man said not a word after that, instead lying facedown as if he had fallen asleep, gripping the bottle by the pillow. The woman rose with the pail in her hands, and the boy followed her out of the cabin. She dumped the dirty water in the river and refilled the pail with fresh water from a jug by the tackle box. Afterward she poured in some white powder soap and let the filthy shirt soak in the sun. He saw the net lying coiled in a heap behind the tackle box. White nylon twine. He bent to inspect the twine, the crimping of the lead. They looked good. There was dried mud and broken twigs and dead leaves inside the net. It had a fish stench and smelled like river silt. He lifted the net up and shook it.

This thing's ten feet deep, he said, glancing up at the woman, who was watching him.

Can you handle it?

Yeah. Just have to bury the footrope down there soon after you throw the net.

That thing isn't light, Nam. When it's full of fish, it's a load.

I know. You got bait, ma'am?

Yeah. Under the board. You'll need mud, though. Fresh mud.

I'll get it, and I'll make the bait whenever you're ready.

A merchant boat was docking alongside their boat. The woman looked down at the small, low boat. You can do the bait later, she said. Let's eat now.

She squatted on the deck and called down to the woman vendor. What've you got in those pots?

Mudskipper soup, the vendor said, tipping up her conical palm-leaf hat, and pointed to one silvery tall pot. And this here is red-tailed rasbora porridge. She lifted the lid of the second pot, and a puff of steam rose.

The woman went into the cabin and came back out with a two-decked tin container. For my husband, the woman said, he loves rasbora porridge. She leaned down to hand the container to the vendor, who filled one deck with white rice porridge and the other with rasbora cooked and poached with fish sauce and now looking golden and heavily flecked with ground black pepper. The woman sat down on the thwart, the boy on the tackle box, eating mudskipper soup from clay bowls. The boy blew and slurped the broth that smarted his tongue with its tangy flavor of lemon grass and ground country gooseberry. The woman came over and dropped into his bowl a pinch of sawtooth herb and basil and cinnamon. She said, Stir it before the broth cools. He thanked her. The fresh herbs gave off a heady fragrance once they were soaked in the steaming broth. The fish floated in white chunks, tender in his mouth. The woman rested her spoon on the rim of her bowl.

My husband, she said, he's half gone from his mind since he's got the boils. I don't expect you to like him, but I do expect good work from you.

I hear you, ma'am. He wiped the wetness the steam left around his nose and said, I don't blame him for his bad mood. How long has he had boils?

Couple weeks, she said as she spooned some broth from the bowl and sipped. They'd start out like mosquito bites. All over his back. They itched so bad I had to rub and scrape his back with a hot towel. And a couple days later they'd grow big, and you could see green pus in them. He said when they were full of pus, they hurt all the way to his head. He drinks most of the time, I guess to numb the pain. He goes through three, four shirts a day. They're all soaked with pus. And if I don't wash them and his back right away, then you saw what happened. He'd be covered with flies in there. He can't go anywhere. Such a shame. Well, I called on a monk once, hoping he'd do something holy to save my husband.

He glanced up toward the cabin and back at her. What's a monk have to do with this?

Some malevolent spirit could've caused this to my husband. That was my thinking. So, the monk came and chanted and left.

What? He didn't do nothing fancy?

No. He said a man's karma reaps its deserving retributions, and no one, not even the Buddha, could change that. He said he could pray only for my husband's karmic offenses. Praying could help dissolve some of a man's offenses, he said.

What he needs is a good doctor, ma'am.

I thought so, too. I've got the name of this doctor. They said he's good.

Then take your husband there to see him.

I'm going to. He's a day from here. Going south as we tend our business.

On our fishing route?

Yes. But we'll be at Black Carp Run before dawn tomorrow. See how well we'll do before we move further south.

She smiled as she stirred her bowl. Her teeth were even, white, and her dimpled smile made him feel at home. As he watched her profile, her shapely neck, above which her hair was knotted in a ball, he thought she had the prettiest neck he'd ever seen.

2

They went on south. During the day she would help him make bait. Sometimes her husband would sit shirtless in the sun, watching them. He claimed sunlight killed bacteria. So, when his boils broke, he'd sit out in the sun till all the blood and pus on his back dried up in blackish red and darkish green streaks. The boy would smell a stench in the breeze.

Early mornings when the boy brought up fresh catch, the woman would pick the best kinds and, with the hand net, lift them up from the cargo hold and drop them into a wax-paper-lined creel. He'd watch her carry the heavy creel by the cane handle on her way to the town's market, walking with even steps, her hips swinging, her hair tucked neatly in a polka-dotted kerchief. He found himself gazing at her till she was gone up a street, still empty at first light. Nights when he was done with the last hauling, he'd scrub himself in the river and then come up for supper, most of the time with only her, while the husband sequestered himself in his own quarters. They would eat under the light of the storm lantern, hearing the fish in the cargo hold thumping and fighting one another in that confined space that held barely enough water for their survival. Late at night, she'd go bathing in the river. He'd lie awake, listening to the gentle sound of water she poured on her body, away from the lantern light, where water was chest high, cool, and cloaked in blackness. When she came up, lowering her head to enter the domed cabin, she was a dark figure save the whiteness of her towel-wrapped head. He'd keep still and find sleep hard to come by in the scent of her body soap. Once, he heard the husband coming into their section while she was still in the water. He could feel the man's presence next to him, squatting on the floorboard and smelling odorous. The boils had spread to his buttocks, so he could barely sit. She came in, parting the entrance curtain, and stopped. The man said, You changed your clothes out there? And she said, Yeah, what's with it? He half rose as he moved backward into his section. Next time, he said, change in my place so I can see you. She did, since then.

3

One morning they came to the river town where the doctor lived. While the boy stayed back on the boat, making bait for the evening, the woman and her husband went to see the town doctor. By the time the boy had finished making the bait on their docked boat, the man and the woman returned. The woman picked up the kitchen utensils from under the floorboard and moved to the prow, on the downwind side, and began cooking lunch. The man stood before the cabin's entrance, smoking a cigarette and looking over the water now hazy with the white heat of noon. The boy threw him a quick glance and went to drag the net across the floor so he could clean out the debris caught inside and between the meshes. He felt the man's eyes following him, so he looked up toward the man, who was still standing in one place, one hand in his jacket pocket, the other cupping the cigarette for one last drag.

Sir, the boy said, anything else you want me to do?

If I make you a list, the man said, flicking the butt over the gunwale, you won't find it challenging anymore. Yeah, there're plenty of work to be done around here. Boat needs to be in tiptop shape all the time. Supplies at hand. He plugged a fresh cigarette between his lips, ran his forefinger across the deep scar on his lower lip to his chin like it was a strand of weed stuck there. I want you to take care of the spark plugs, grease, oil, kerosene. All that. Don't let weeds or any crap build up on the bottom of the boat. Clean them off often as you can. Any wear and tear on the boat, I'll fix them. And I want you just to haul in fish. But I need you to do more hauling now. A lot more. That's what I used to do.

The boy shook loose dead leaves still damp in the net. What d'you mean a lot more, sir? he said, eyeing the man.

Tell you what. I used to fill that cargo hold there with fish overnight. I mean filled to the hatch. Yeah. Then I filled the net and just let that damn thing soak in the river till morning. If you ask how we've been doing, I'll tell you. Our catch has been dropped by half.

The boy nodded. He knew he could handle it. He used to do it for his uncle, who'd make several hauls a night, as long as he still saw the bubbles the fish made on the water.

Make more bait for tonight, the man said.

Okay, sir, the boy said. I'll go into town to get more supplies, then.

And fuel. It's half empty.

I know, sir. I meant to buy more gasoline today, when I'm done with this cleaning.

You buy gasoline where it's sold cheap. Whatever town. Remember them. You go back to them. Got me? That's how I do my business. That'll save money.

Yessir. I'll remember that.

Did your uncle do that?

The boy turned to look at the man. Do what, sir?

Don't try to be smart now. You know what I mean.

I don't want to talk about my uncle.

You haven't answered my question.

I won't. The boy stood up. He looked at the man, who locked eyes with him. He saw a face hardened by weather and hate. He saw the swollen red boil on the cheek and felt his dislike for the man. The man blew a stream of smoke toward him.

You want to work here, don't you?

Yessir.

Then do what I ask you.

I'll do whatever you ask me, sir, that's part of my job. But you leave my family out.

Fuck, the man said, throwing the cigarette butt down at his bare foot and grinding it with his heel. Just then the woman came through the cabin and stepped in between the two of them. Let's eat, she said. It's been a long morning.

I'll eat later, the boy said, sitting down on the stern by the net. I'm about done with this.

The woman wanted to say something but stopped. Then she and the man made their way through the cabin to the prow, from where the boy could hear her restrained voice and the man's sudden curses.

Later she brought him a bowl of steamed white rice to eat with a bowl of goby soup. She said, When you're done with lunch, we'll go to town and get supplies. He thanked her and sat in the sun, eating his lunch. The rice was still warm, still fragrant. He scooped it and dropped a few spoonfuls into the bowl of soup. Coral-colored balls of shrimp floated in the broth, and a thick cut of goby sank in the bottom of the bowl. He felt deep down a touch of her kindness, and he was grateful for that. There were greens of sweet leaf and vine spinach, and their delicate taste seeped into his tongue, and, blowing and chewing, he forgot what just happened between him and the man.

After he was done with lunch, he thought of taking his bowl to the prow to clean in a pan she used for washing dishes. Then he decided not to. Going through the cabin would mean he would have to look at the man again, and he didn't feel like talking to him at all. The woman came out, a wicker basket hooked on her forearm.

You haven't heard the last of him, she said to him.

I'll do what he asks, the boy said. I told him that.

I heard you. Well, we were both stressed out. Doctor's fees got him worried.

Aren't you worried?

Not worried. Scared. What if we run out of money?

Treatment costs that much, ma'am?

Yeah. Not a one-time deal, you understand? His first treatment starts tomorrow morning. Then skip one day and back again.

The boy said nothing. He knew they also had to pay for the boat. His uncle's boat was even bigger than theirs, with more luxury, which kept him working round the clock. The woman looked up at him, scratching the side of her face lightly. How many runs can you do tonight? she said.

Till I'm tired.

Okay. She said nothing for a while, then, You know when to stop, don't you?

4

Another week passed. The boy had seen less and less of the man during the day, because the man spent most of it at the doctor's house. On a day when the man returned to the boat at noon to rest and when the woman was in town, the boy raised the cargo hatch and, after looking over the catch from the evening before, finally scooped up a good-sized carp. He placed the carp in a wicker basket lined with wax paper and, not bothering to tell the man where he'd be heading, left the boat and went to town.

He saw the doctor's shiny black Peugeot parked beside the house. The noon sun shone on its paint, and the glare hurt his eyes. The car looked like a historic object on exhibit in a museum. He chose not to enter through the front door, where inside there was always a crowd. She had told him to give the fish to the doctor in person and ask him to ice it as soon as he could. The boy went down the side of the house to a door at the end and took the stairs to the second-floor office. He'd never been up here before. He walked along the floor, which was tiled in a mosaic, and past closed, dark brown doors. One, two, three, not knowing which door to knock. *Does he live here, too?* He heard low voices, muffled. A chair scratched on the tiled floor. He leaned against the wall and felt it tremble as if someone had suddenly bumped against it. Then her voice: Please don't do this; this is not right. He heard a man's voice. A slurred tone. The wall shook again like something was banged against it. He stood, his guts churning. Suddenly the second door flung open. She came out, buttoning the front of her pink blouse. She saw him. Her eyes might not have recognized him at first, but at the same time he knew it had just hit her who he was. She quickly brushed a stray strand of hair off her brow, her kerchief askew on her head. The doctor stopped at the doorway when he saw him. Neither he nor the woman spoke. The boy stepped up past the woman, who chose not to turn around, and set the basket at the doctor's feet.

She . . . well . . . and her husband wanted you to have this, the boy said, adding the husband part on the fly.

The doctor looked down at the lidded wicker basket and back at the boy. Yeah, he said woodenly.

You need to put it in ice, sir, the boy said, stepping backward to where the woman was.

Yeah, the doctor said, combing his hair with his fingers. Then, as they were leaving, he said, What's in there to ice?

The boy looked back. A fish, sir. Black carp.

They hurried down the narrow stairs together, he pressing his body against the stucco wall to give her room and then following her, looking at her bare neck, at the fine downy hair that curled prettily at the base of the hairline. *What's that damn doctor doing in there?* But he said nothing to her, and she was quiet as a mouse till they walked side by side down the street, passing under overhanging canopies that shaded the sidewalk.

My husband shouldn't know about this, she said, composed now, and he noticed her rouged lips. *What was she doing in his office?*

Yes, ma'am.

They kept walking in the direction of the waterfront till she stopped at a cross street. I have something I need to take care of, she said, dabbing her perspiring cheeks with the heel of her hand.

What is it that you need to do? he asked before he realized he shouldn't have.

I need to wire money to the bank. She shrugged. Boat payment.

Do you . . . he said, lost for words, I mean, is he gonna see that doctor again after . . . what happened today?

I'm afraid so. Just because he's healing. Does it sound like a curse to you?

Healing, is he? That's news.

But good news, she said. His boils go flat now—most of them do. But he's got new ones, too. Not many. The old ones, they've stayed drained and flat. And, thank Heaven, he can sleep now, even on his back.

A few nights before she had come back up from the river after a late-night bath and, yes, the man was soundly asleep. She sat on the thwart while she changed out of her wet clothes, so she wouldn't wake him. The boy thought back to that night when the man ordered her to do this routine in his cabin and not outside. His thought stopped the moment he saw her work herself out of her blouse. She raised her arms behind her head, twisting her wet hair to squeeze water out. Her body was so white it cut a milky figure against the darkness, a body as compact as a black carp. He knew his own thought and was disturbed with guilt.

On a day he was going in to have the treatment, her husband asked for the payment money just before he left the boat. She told him that, for the sake of convenience, she'd arranged with the doctor to debit each visit's fee to her account.

When the husband came back before noon, he told her he had to go in only for another week, then it was all over. There had been only one new boil in the last seven days, and the doctor assured him that his ordeal was about to end. At noon the boy returned with fresh supplies of bait and found only the man on the boat. The air smelled rich with cooked rice. The man was sitting shirtless outside the cabin, skinning a zigzag eel on a large cutting board. The eel must have been two feet long, brown-bodied, striped lengthwise with several zigzag bars in mocha brown. It was caught in the net the previous evening, this bottom dweller.

The man scooped the skin and dropped it into a trash bag, wiped his hands with an old newspaper, and then plugged a cigarette between his lips. The boy dropped his gaze as he saw the man look toward him at the stern.

You making more bait for tonight? the man said, blowing smoke upward.

Yeah.

This one here's a good catch. You like eel?

I've eaten it before. How you cook it is what makes it good, I think.

You just watch, then tell me later if it's good.

I believe you, sir. You must be good at it.

You're damn right. The man took a deep drag, his eyes closed to slits as he looked at the boy. Prisoners of war got shit to eat, he said. Whatever we could lay our hands on we cooked like hungry fiends. Rats, snakes, turtles, skinks. But this eel here, hell, if you got this back then, it's worth more than gold.

Yeah. The boy nodded and kept busy.

The man puffed on his cigarette as he slit the eel lengthwise with the tip of the knife, cleaned out the gut, which he gathered with the knife blade and shoved into the trash bag, careful not to spill too much of the eel's blood, then cut it into finger-length chunks. Without looking at him, the boy could hear the steady chopping, then the smells of garlic, onion wafted across, raw and sharp. The trash bag tied down, a rag in hand, the man cleaned around his work area to his satisfaction and then set up a terracotta pot to boil water. He smoked and waited, watching the boy, who had just finished one batch of bait and dropped them into the jute bag.

The sun glared on the deck, drying up dark wet spots one after another. The man touched his face, his cheek. The last stubborn boil there was now flat. A glance at him and the boy remembered those boils in their grotesque sizes now gone, perhaps only their mild presence still there to torture the man's memory. The water hissed. He lifted the lid and dropped in black peppercorns, a handful of bay leaves, and then stirred a good pinch of turmeric in a bowl of fish sauce till its amber color turned saffron-yellow and then just a dull dark brown. He poured the cup into the pot, waited till the pungent turmeric aroma rose, making him sneeze once then twice, and then turned down the flame and carefully dropped the eel, still full of blood inside, into the simmering liquid.

The boy washed his hands in the river and came up, as he was asked, to join the man for lunch. They sat with their legs folded under them and the pot between them. The eel simmered red. The boy felt it burn on his tongue, his palate, and so he held a mouthful of warm rice in his mouth to absorb the searing heat. The man was dousing his rice with the cooking liquid in burned caramel color, and he, blowing and chewing noisily, tapped his chopsticks against the bowl's rim to shake loose the clumped rice. He drank from his liquor bottle and licked his red, greasy lips, running his tongue over the raw-looking scar.

Where's she? the boy said.

I thought you knew, the man said, burping.

I don't.

Oh yeah? You must've known her routine well by now. Am I right?

The man's tone of voice made the boy stop eating. He checked the man's expression and saw a face flushed from the heat, liquor, and what he'd just cooked and eaten. Except the eyes. Always harboring a baleful look.

Should we save some for her? he asked the man.

What d'you think? Should we?

The boy shrugged.

Means what? The man's raised pitch made his grin sinister.

I'll save some for her, sir, if you want me to.

Dump it. Leftover tastes like shit.

Well, she might not like eel, anyway.

What else she likes?

Again, the boy shrugged. He put down the half-empty bowl.

Tell me what she likes? the man said and then took a long swig from the bottle.

What she likes ain't none of my business, sir.

She likes you, don't she?

What?

Have you been screwing my wife? The man blurted, spitting out a piece of food.

Sir?

Have you been fucking her while I was away?

The boy's chest felt heavy, like someone was pressing down on it. He felt ridiculed. He didn't like it. Sir, he said, leaning forward on the elbow that rested on his thigh, you'll regret what you just said.

I thought you'll be the fucker who might regret.

I ain't no fucker if that's what's been bothering you. She's a good woman. I have no need to say nothing more.

The man watched him. Cold, calculating eyes. The boy looked him in the face, his expression hardened, his eyes unblinking. Finally, the man stroked his chin, reached for the bottle and gave it to him. Here, he said.

The boy tipped back his head and drank. Then he wiped the grease off the bottleneck and blew through his lips. He peered across at the man, who was looking at him, but the boy could see that his mind was somewhere else. Sir, he said, what'd she do that made you say something like that?

The man chewed on his lower lip pensively, the menace bleached off his face, but something dark now brooded there. Fuck if I know, he said, cycling his jaw. I thought I knew women.

❖

Late that night he heard her coming up from the river. He could hear her wet steps outside the cabin. Then stillness. In his mind she was sitting on the thwart, unbuttoning her blouse, wet and stuck to her body, and then letting it fall in a heap at her feet. He heard water dripping onto the deck and, with his eyes closed, saw her arms flung back behind her head to squeeze water out of her hair, and felt that unclean desire to get up and peep through the entrance, to see again what he'd seen. Did she know that he was only ten feet away?

But he didn't get up. She must've washed the red lipstick off her lips by now, and its red had stayed on his mind since she returned to the boat in the early afternoon. She brought back with her the household supplies, and she smelled of perfume, just a whiff of it, when she brushed past him. Business was brisk in the afternoon. Customers came and went. He asked her if she had eaten lunch, and she said no. He said nothing afterward, remembering the red of her lipstick.

She came into the cabin, soundless. As she turned her body to sit down on the plank bed, her hair swinging round her neck, he felt a drop of water on his face. She wore a salmon-on-pink blouse, the pink almost as pale as her skin. She sat on the bed for one brief moment, the air tinged with minty soap, and then a breeze fluttered the entrance curtain and the cabin smelled like the river, of things long immersed in the water, of mud, of flatsedge and of water chestnut.

He knew he didn't hate her. It was something else.

5

He made at least twenty hauls the next day, and he hauled in the evening till the cargo hold was packed with fish. She kept splashing water into the cargo hold. When it was full, she asked him to stop for the night. He didn't answer and went down for one last haul and came up dizzy and weak. A drizzle fell. He stood looking down into the dark water, trying to get his breathing again, while behind him she cooked ramen. The night was cool and starless, and the wind blew light rain against the lantern..

C'mon, it's ready, she said.

Her hair was damp, no longer curled. He hated the curls in her hair when she went to town in the morning and while her husband was in the doctor's office. She curled her hair with the iron curlers that she heated over the brazier, and those locks of hair bounced like they had springs as she walked. Now, seeing her without lipstick, her hair straight and wetly matted down on her round forehead, he felt closer to her.

He ate while she sat with her hands in her lap. Why don't you eat? he said, wiping the corner of his mouth.

I don't feel hungry.

We've got lots of fish today.

Don't we? She turned her head as she heard the banging the fish made against the hatch. As she turned back, some rain droplets fell in her eyes and made her blink. He felt in his throat the thickness which he knew too well whenever he was near her. He didn't like that feeling, but he couldn't help it. Then, as he drank down the broth, he thought of what the husband said earlier in the day and felt sick.

She gave out her hand to take the bowl from him, and, as she refilled it he looked toward the curtained entrance of the cabin, imagining the man in there still awake, lying in torment with the thought of infidelity. He could sense something dark coming, like the way he could tell about a coming rain on the plain from the colors of sky and clouds.

About tomorrow, he said, putting the bowl down, I'm set to move on.

That drew a surprised stare from her. Why'd you want to do that? she said, her tone resigned as if she already knew.

He's doing okay now. You won't need me around.

You mean my husband? Well.

She watched him finish the bowl, leaving it clean, and then stood up and walked to the gunwale where the net was tied to the peg by its landline. It was so quiet she could hear the fish snapping at bubbles on the surface of water. The water was black, and the lantern shone on it where the net lay spread. Beyond it, downriver, as far as the other bank, there was nothing but blackness and distant lights. A good stretch away from their boat on this side of the river, she could see a lantern light at a jetty, and as she listened to the stillness, she could hear the scraping sound of a boat just coming in over the graveled landing.

Another week, and the town and the river that ran through it would be nothing but a memory. She could never forget it even if she wanted to. Not the small room where the shades were drawn, the mosaic tiles cool underfoot, the ceiling fan forever spinning unhurriedly. Sometimes she would feel the air it stirred breathe across her bare back, sometimes on her breasts as she fixed her eyes on the white ceiling, waiting for it to be over. The room was so quiet, save the doctor's laborious breathing, his back-and-forth motion over her that caused the creaking of the bed. It was so quiet she could hear voices now and then from a floor below, from the waiting room full of pa- tients, and next to it the treatment room where her husband was lying face down on a raised bed, a nurse tending to his boils that had lately shown signs of remission. All the sums she and he owed to that man would be phantom numbers. It was so because of her own choosing.

Well, the boy said, coming up to the gunwale, I'm gonna pull in that net now.

She moved toward him and touched the line, feeling the fine rain on her hand. Let me help, she said, and pulled.

Get in front, I'll give you some slack.

She braced her back against him, her feet against the side of the boat, pulling with both hands, as he pulled with his arms outside of hers, both seeing the net rise slowly, heavily till it hung over the water. She held the line while he looped the end of it round the peg, and slowly she let go of it, and they heard the net plop into the water.

Biggest catch, don't you think? she said, smiling.

So damn heavy. Don't know what I'd do if I were by myself.

I'm going to pick the best one tomorrow, she said, wiping her face with her hand. Just for us.

Plenty good ones to pick from.

Depends on what you want to eat. Tell me.

A black carp. He didn't know at first why he said that. Yet its compact fleshy body had always stayed on his mind.

I'll cook us a meal with it. Caramel carp.

You're a good cook. He nodded at her dimpled smile. It'll be my last meal with you and him.

I know. I won't forget.

Me neither. Well, you might forget this town. But not the good moments we could remember together.

Yes.

He gazed at her long enough that she glanced away.

I guess you're right, she said.

The Yin-Yang Market

I sip my black coffee, peering up at her. I have offered her a cup of café *phin*—slow-drip coffee. She palms the cup with both hands. Head lowered. The cup raised to her lips. She sips gingerly, her brow furrowed.

"It's so peaceful around here," she says, her partially tilted face leaning into the morning light which glints on the fine downy hair at the base of her neck.

"We live a slow life here. I'm sure you'll forget everything by the time you go back home."

"I keep the things I learn—things I select to remember."

"Like what?"

She shrugs. "Like the drip coffee," she says. "And I'm fascinated with those rivers and canals around here. And the lives that depend on them."

I catch her gaze over the cup's rim, serene eyes, elongated and pretty, the brow uncreased this time; perhaps she is now getting used to the bitter taste of the café *phin*, this orphan child having been displaced to grow up into a comely girl, always exuding liveliness and consideration.

She came to my inn in the Mekong Delta with her American mother, who adopted her in 1974, when she was five years old. She's eighteen now.

She took many photographs during her first trip to the U Minh Forest with her mother and me. Her young mind sponged up things, and I felt lively in her presence. Yet I could never think of her as a Vietnamese.

"Do you feel like a foreigner to your own birthplace?"

"I don't feel foreign to Vietnam. I remember the place where I came from. It looks just like the places around here."

"Where? You've never told me."

"You never asked, *chú*."

She called me *uncle*, with a lilt in her voice. "Where then?"

"Plain of Reeds. In the delta too."

"I know where it is. What do you remember?"

"The floods that came every year after summer. The canals that took you to the big rivers. The mangrove trees in the plain. The stilt houses along the rivers."

"And you left Vietnam when you were five?"

"Yes." She recrosses her legs, her finger tracing the sewn-on rose on her jeans. "Do you remember those empty stilts along the riverbank? Just stilts on the mud bank with no houses on them?"

"What about them?"

"The other day, I photographed them. I thought, what happened to the houses? Stilts but no houses. I wanted to ask you, but you were busy talking with my mother . . . ."

"They were destroyed during the war. Just ruins now. Like people. Died, or moved away."

"I used to see them when I went to the riverbank with the nuns. I grew up in an orphanage run by the nuns."

I sip. "Do you want to visit that orphanage?"

"It's no longer there. Some foreign company bought the surrounding land a few years back for business development."

"How do you know?"

"I keep in touch with the head nun. But recently I lost her. She said she'd write me when she knew where they would relocate the orphanage. She sent a photograph of the old orphanage with a church behind it. I'll never forget the white steeple of that church."

Drawn into her story, I leaned forward as she continued. "I got lost in the marketplace one day, separated from the head nun. I was scared, but I didn't cry. I found my way out of the market and took the road we came in on, remembering the scenery, and kept walking until I saw the tower, and then

I knew I wasn't lost anymore."

"How old were you at that time?"

"Barely five."

She tells me about the place she came from: the one-story, L-shaped, tin-roofed, mango wood-walled house that sheltered nine orphans, four to ten years old. Behind the orphanage and the white-steepled church was a fishpond, and behind that a plot overgrown with banana trees whose fronds the nuns would cut and wash and later use to wrap food. In that banana grove, caught by a sudden late-afternoon thunderstorm, the head nun held her tight against her bosom, both crouching from the lashing rain. The nun broke the fronds at the stems to screen themselves and took off her scarf and wrapped it around the little girl's head. A streak of lightning struck at ground level, like a sudden flash out of a mirror. Then followed an ear-splitting thunderclap. The girl plugged her ears as another crash shook the ground. She heard the wind ripping through the banana trees, and out in the open the hummingbird trees bent and snapped back, and leaves flew fluttering like birds. The pebble-sized raindrops pelted her face and the banana fronds and pockmarked the pond's water. A white flash hit the ground across the pond, searing a hummingbird tree in midsection. The tree snapped. The girl could smell the burned smoke. She said, sobbing, into the nun's chest, "I don't want to be here," and the nun cradled her in her arms. "We'd better stay for a little while. I promise nothing shall hurt you, my dear." The girl inhaled the nun's warm, sweaty smell. Suddenly the nun squirmed, saying, "I've got something under my blouse." The nun eased the girl off her and unbuttoned her blouse. The little girl stared at a black thing against the nun's chest. A caterpillar. Across the air suddenly flashed a jagged line. Then an explosion so loud her ears rang. She mashed her face in the nun's bosom, the nun shielding her now with the open front of her blouse. Eyes shut, she heard the nun cooing. She felt the flesh warm and abundantly soft, smelling like wet leaves, and she felt raindrops trickling down to her lips. The thunder came less and less often now and soon rolled into the distance. Then just the rain clattered on the leaves, the smoky smell now gone from the air, and it felt dank in the wind. The nun gently pulled her away from her chest. "It's safe now, child," she said. The girl wiped rain from her cheeks, following the nun's fingers trying to match a button against its buttonhole. She kept gazing at the ample flesh of the nun's bosom, then at a pink ridge of a scar across her breasts. She didn't ask. But the sight of the scar stayed with her.

At dawn, she would rise to help the nun in the rear kitchen, sitting on her heels on the packed-earth floor, stacking coconut leaves, then stripping the leaves from the stiff midribs. The nun would light the dry leaves and feed them into the hearth, and, when the flames spurted, she poured a bowlful of rice husks into the fire. The hearth crackled, the husks exhaled acrid fumes, and the flames rose in blue tongues. She would save the midribs and the stems for the nun. The children would tie the stems together into a fan-shaped bundle into which they would fit a handle. That was how they made brooms. The nun would let her pour rice flour evenly onto a white gauze that screened a wide-bottomed pot, the square cloth held down drum-tight by four bricks, the pot steaming with boiling water. She would spread the rice flour—a creamy white mixture of sugar and coconut extract and sesame seeds—in a round layer, and the nun lidded it with a cane cover. The girl would stare at the rice crepe after the lid was removed, the crepe so thin, opaque white. The nun would slide a wide wooden blade under the crepe, lifting it gently so it hung flapping, round-shaped and wet and paper-thin, and then drop it on a palm-woven sieve. As the nun bent to scoop up rice husks with a bowl to add to the fire, the girl could see the nun's breasts through her collarless blouse, the long scar, braidlike, across her chest. They had to use up the flour just before the sun had burned off the morning mist, so they could put out the sieves for the crepes to dry in the sun. By noon the crepes would be dry, and the children would take the sieves back in and stack the crepes by tens, tie them down, and wrap them in brown papers. Later a nun would carry them to the local market and sell them on consignment.

Then the flood season came. One morning after a three-day rain, she woke and saw floodwaters rising to the door-steps. By noon, the water was coming into the house. She could no longer see the long table where they ate, but only the tops of the straight-backed chairs. The nuns put the children in three canoes, the long, slender canoes always tied to the trunks of the hummingbird trees behind the house, and now with the children safely together, all bunched up in their clear plastic raincoats, the nuns began paddling away. The plain behind the house was a steely gray sheet of water brimming to the horizon. River hemp bushes, yellow flowering, marked the boundaries between landowners' paddy fields in the gray water. She could tell where they were by the familiar sights: clumps of half-submerged flat sedge fringing a pond, the pond now rising with cloudy water. The head nun handed her the short paddle and reached out for a blue water lily. She gave the girl the flower and took the paddle back. The girl asked if the nun's arms were tired from rowing, for the nun had taught her how to row with the *cây dam*, much shorter than an oar, made of thingan wood, polished and always light. The nun shook her head and rowed on. They would stop when they spotted small crabs taking shelter on a floating quilt of water hyacinths, so the children could pick them up and play with the mottled-brown crabs that always camouflaged themselves with the color patterns of their surroundings. Sometimes late in the afternoon when the water stopped rising, the nuns rest-ed with the canoes leaning against the crown of a young bush-willow with its trunk, at least two meters tall, submerged in water. Neighbored by nothing but gray sky and white water, the nuns began setting the fishing poles, fitting each butt into a bored hole in the upper side of the canoe. The poles arched over the water, and the lines plumbed the water's depth. The children ate rice balls out of their banana leaves. The girl, too, chewed a rice ball, long-grained and sticky, with ground, salted sesame seeds. She could taste its roasted aroma. Her mind grew dreamy. They caught several perches. The head nun, one hand holding the line, held up a perch, its dusky-green body quaking in her hand, as the children gawked. The nun told them this fish could walk. The children giggled and asked how. "It uses its tail and fins," the nun said, "to move over land." The girl remembered that. The walking perch. They rowed on, the nuns stopping at times to untangle feathery roots of water lettuce from their paddles. Passing an earthen dike barely jutting above the water, the head nun pointed toward a paling of cajeput stakes, closely joined, and asked if anyone knew what the barrier was for. The girl said it was to catch fish. The nun said, "You're very smart, child, but this isn't a fish weir." As the canoes came alongside the wet, battered-looking paling, the nun told them to look down into the water. "A fish weir," she said, "has stakes with a fair distance between them, and with horizontal wattling between stakes to trap fish. Do you see any wattling down there?" The children said no. The nun said, "This paling is to protect the dike from further water damage. You as my children live your protected lives in the orphanage, but out here people's lives depend on the waterways, and sometimes water encroaches their habitats, and so their work never ends, the year-round mending of things in the delta."

Beyond the dike, they came around a hummock rising above the water like an elephant back. The nuns shipped the paddles, docked the canoes, and led the children up the knoll. Twilight was falling, spreading a fan-shaped glow across the water, luminous water swelling to the gray sky. They walked under cajeput trees into the gloom harbored by their damp leaves, now black and dripping rainwater. In a clearing, a stilt hut sat three feet above the ground. Flanking the steps were

clay vats, lidded and waist high. Beneath the stairs was parked
a skiff covered in a moss-green plastic sheet. An old man sat
outside the hut on the bottom step. The girl recognized him.
He was the gap-toothed janitor who helped fix things around
the orphanage. He built all the furniture, the tables and
chairs, and one time made a pen nib for her. She remembered
one morning seeing him on the doorsteps pounding a leaf of
gray metal cut out from a milk can. She sat by him. "Making
you a new pen nib as she told me to," he said, referring to the
head nun, as he cut the metal into a sliver. "So you can write
again," he said. "You write, eh? How old are you?" She said,
"Four." He looked her up and down. "I don't even know my
age," he said, "but I can count with my fingers." With the tip
of his tongue protruding between his lips, he began hammer-
ing the metal sliver.

Now he raised his hand to greet the nuns. So, this is where
he lives, she thought. In the ash-blue twilight beyond the
clearing where bushes grew wild, she saw humps of graves
plagued by needle grass and false daisy. The white, small flowers glimmered. She'd seen these same flowers around the orphanage. When they followed the old man up the steps and
into the hut, she could hear from behind the hut the hens
clucking and the throaty gargles the ducks made in their pens.
The old man lit the kerosene lamp hanging from a hook on a
maroon post. The hut glowed eerily in the trembling light, the
corners full of shadows. The floor, lined with shorn boles of
cajeput, glowed with a bone shine. Next to the lamp hung a
lute, odd-shaped, its body as round as a coconut. The hearth
crackled with a strong fire, the old man feeding the fire with
cajeput wood, then dropping dry cajeput leaves on the flames,
giving off a foul smell. "Keeps out the mosquitos," he told the
children sitting around the hearth. The girl followed a nun
outside to get away from the smelly smoke. The nun knelt on
a flagstone by a vat and began gutting a perch with a knife.
Watching the nun prepare the fish, the girl heard heavy wings
up in the dark tangles of cajeput trees. She looked up and saw
white storks and white egrets coming home to roost for the

night. The twilight stillness was broken by the incessant, raw beating of their wings.

The head nun came out of the hut. "Are you hungry, child?" The girl nodded. The nun said, "We're staying here until the water goes down, then we go back home and start cleaning up. I'll be back soon." The girl asked, "Where are you going?" The nun pointed toward the gloom beyond the clearing. The girl saw the humps of graves, now just blurred swells. "What's there?" she asked. The nun looked down at the ground. "My daughter's grave," she said. The girl said nothing but felt a deep separation of mother and child. "Can I go with you?" The nun patted her head. "Yes, child." And they walked beneath the rustle of wings to the graveyard.

The small grave sat on the rim of the knoll, which sloped into an overflowing canal. The ground felt soft around the grave, matted with yellow-flowering plant. "Aren't they pretty?" the nun said, bending to pluck a handful of the flowers. The girl asked, "What's this plant?" The nun gathered the long-stemmed flowers, each shaped like a yellow-colored eyeball with a red dot in its center. "*Co the*," the nun said. "Like its name says. It tastes like mint, strong enough to numb your gums." The nun placed the small bouquet of toothache plant on the grave. The girl gazed down at the restless water, rushing headlong as though the earth were tipped on its side, a dank smell rising from the canal. Then came a sudden sound of wings. A pond heron shot up from the canal, coming over them so low she could see its brown-streaked plumage as it sailed into the dark vault of trees. Despite the tumult, the nun stood with head bowed, forming words of prayer. She crossed herself. The girl imagined a presence in the grave. Forever out here in the heat and rain. "Why did she die?" she asked. The nun took a sharp breath and slowly exhaled. "She drowned in the flood." The girl remembered stories about drowned people who would float back up, bloated and blue-cold, after three days in the deep. The nun said softly, "Since then, I've been always prepared for the flood, so you children will always be safe with me." She patted the girl's head. "She was only your age." The girl noticed the small grave, small enough to be overlooked had it not sat alone on the tip of the knoll. "It's so small," she said. The nun said, "It is small, my child. Just a grave. Nothing in it. I could not recover her body. But I want to remember her, that's my wish." The nun squeezed the child's hand. The damp smell like vegetation came up from the water below reminded the child that she would always be safe on high, dry ground like this. Walking back toward the hut, the nun said, "She had eyes like you. You have the Virgin Mary's eyes, my child."

From inside the hut came a thick smell of smoked fish. The fire in the hearth made shadows in the doorway. Leaning against a broken vat, the girl stood watching the head nun cleaning her neck. Then unbuttoning her blouse, the nun began washing her chest. In the yellow glimmer the girl gazed at the flesh. When the hand went away, the flesh was bare and milky, and across the flesh was the long ridgelike scar.

She puts her cup down on the windowsill, raises herself up on her arms and sits comfortably on the sill with her legs dangling. It is bright outside, and the breeze is warm coming into the room, and you can smell the wild grass and the old peat soil.

I try to picture her as a child. I imagine hearing her gentle voice, speaking in Vietnamese. "Maybe someday you'll find the nun," I say.

"I hope so," Chi Lan says. "I will come back here."

"You will?" I cough, reaching for the cigarette pack on the table.

"You cough a lot, *chú*. Maybe you should see a doctor."

"Maybe I should."

"How long have you smoked?"

"As long as I've drunk black coffee."

"Well, how long then?"

"All the vices I picked up when I was fifteen."

"You were fifteen going on fifty."

I chuckle. My throat feels raspy. This morning, she wears a scarlet, collarless blouse. A lock of black hair curls over her neckline, held by a button, opens out in a small V.

I looked at her neckline, and something returned to my mind. "The nun," I say, "how did she have such a scar?"

"From a rape."

I draw back. "During the war?"

"Yes. She fought him, and he cut her with a bowie knife."

"How terrible. Who . . . ?"

"An American marine—when they raided her village in the Plain of Reeds, where she ran her orphanage."

"Her daughter was the result of the rape?"

Chi Lan nods.

I raise my cup to my lips. "When was the last time you saw her?"

"After she agreed to have my American mother adopt me. I cried when she told me. She held me a long time, and when I stopped crying, she told me it was the right thing to do. For me. That I would have a future that would allow me to grow as a free spirit.

"That night she woke me before midnight and told me to come with her. She said, 'I want you to see something that you will never see again once you leave Vietnam.' I asked, 'What is it you want me to see?' She said, 'A marketplace.' I said, 'But it's night now.' She said, 'Yes, child, it's the hour that matters.'"

I interrupt her. "Do you mean *Cho Âm Duong*?"

"Yes." She flicks a smile. "I had the words translated in my head before I told you, because I didn't want to say it incorrectly."

"I know what it is."

"Do you? What is it then?"

"We had it in the North. It's hard to explain to outsiders what it is."

"I want to know if we're talking about the same thing."

"In the North, in this particular village in Bac Ninh Province in the Red River Delta, there was this marketplace called *Cho Âm Duong.* It opened only once a year, on the fifth day of the Lunar New Year."

"*Chú . . . .*" She cuts in.

I pause, peering at her, and take another sip of coffee.

"The nun," she says, perking up, "was born in the North and came to the South in 1954, when Vietnam was separated into North and South. She said the people who started this *yin-yang* market in the South were northerners, the anti-communist Catholics." She stops, smiles at me. "Now you can go on."

"It makes sense," I say, drawn by her gaze. "And so, they said the location of this marketplace used to be a battlefield centuries ago in the feudal time. So many had died their tragic deaths there the *yin* force just shrouds the place."

"Yes, *Chú.*" She palms her cup in her lap. "On that day, just past midnight, the market opened. Nobody carried a lamp. In the dark, people came to buy things. Then the market closed before first light."

I propped my chin with my fist and listened as she continued.

"The head nun took me to the market outside our district, near a river. An empty tract of land with stilts standing but no houses atop them. The nun said, 'There used to be a village here ten years ago. In just one day it was gone.' She said the Viet Cong took cover in the village to ambush the Allies, and the Allies counterattacked and shelled it to ash. They all died. The Viet Cong and the innocents."

She sets the cup down. "It was past midnight when we got there. A new hour that began a new day on the fifth of the Lunar New Year. There were no lights. I asked the nun, 'Why is it so dark?' She said, 'Just follow me, child.' So, she held my hand, and we found our way in the dark, walking on bare ground, stepping between people who sat with baskets and bins in front of them. I could hear my footfalls in the stillness. And wisps of voices. I could smell the steam of rice porridge, the rich odor of beef broth they used to brew porridge with. White steamed buns, rice balls, *bánh lá*—the leaf-wrapped dumplings—were laid out on the sieves. The familiar odor of steamed noodles. Finally, the nun found someone. A turbaned woman who sat with a tray at her feet. The nun made me sit between her and the old woman. I bent to see what the old woman had on the tray. 'What are those?' I whispered to the nun. She said into my ear, 'Betel leaves and areca nuts.' She picked up a betel leaf, tore it halfway, and held it to my nose. I winced at the dark, spicy smell. That old janitor always chewed this sort of leaf with a sliver of areca nut. When he grinned, you could see his tongue, and his gums looked as though they were bleeding badly. Now I thought this was some strange market. It was chilly. The nun held me to her side, and I rested my head on her shoulder. People were sitting all over the ground in an eerie stillness. I could smell the river in the breeze, its old muddy smell. The sky was low and moonless. I fell asleep on the nun's shoulder; I don't know for how long. Then someone whispered, someone answered, and I woke. A woman wearing a conical hat was standing before me. She folded a betel leaf into a quid and then worked it into her mouth. Her oyster-gray palm-leaf hat glimmered, covering most of her face; her *bà ba* blouse was so white she seemed to glow. She handed the turbaned woman a coin, then turned and walked away. The whiteness of her blouse sank into the blackness. Like stepping into a dark doorway. There were more people now, shuffling about, indistinct, shapeless, wearing the white *bà ba* blouses, the wide-legged pantaloons. They sat down, eating from the vendors' bowls. I could hear the slurping noise they made. The air felt cold and damp on the skin, a shivering dampness not there before. I snuggled against the nun, and she put her arms around me. *Who are these people? Where'd they come from?* Nobody spoke. It was like seeing things in black and white. Someone came for a betel chew, then another. Older women. When they came, the air would feel colder, like when you open the door, and the damp air comes in after it has rained all night. I fell asleep on the nun's shoulder, and when I woke the market vendors were packing up. Some vendors had lit their kerosene lamps, the glow painting amber lights and shadows on their faces. The turbaned woman had sold out her betel-chew condiments. The nun said something to her, and she began emptying her blouse pockets onto her tray. Wrinkled arrowroot leaves, dried-up banana leaves, holed seashells, pebbles round and square. Like a child's things. 'Why do you carry them in your pockets?' I asked the woman. She looked down into my eyes, about to say something, when the nun said, 'These aren't hers, child. They came from the people who came here to buy things from her.' I said, 'Are they worth anything?' The nun shook her head and said, 'No, child. Themselves they aren't worth anything. But they were money when those who came here paid her and other vendors.' I said, 'But they're not money.' The nun said, 'They were money when those people were here.' Picking up a round pebble, the nun put it in my hand and said, 'This was a coin when they paid her.' She picked up a dried arrowroot leaf and said, 'This was paper money when they gave it to her. You see, child, those people aren't living people, like us. They have been dead for many years now. They came back from their *yin* world into our *yang* world, this marketplace, so they could enjoy again our worldly pleasures for one brief moment. There was no bargaining, no haggling about the prices in this market. They came, bought things, paid for them. It was real money when they paid. The coin money, the paper money. Only after they have left to go back to their *yin* world, the money turned back to its true origins.' The nun patted my head. 'Now, do you understand why I said that you shall never see anything like this again after you leave Vietnam?' I stood looking at the pebble in my hand. A child's thing, like when children play *buy-and-sell*. We'd use seashells, pebbles, cutout papers for money."

A Mute Girl's Yarn

The Swallow

Father told me when I was seven that every Vietnamese name has a meaning. My name is Hai Yen. Tran Thi Hai Yen. My first name, Hai Yen, means the swallow, a seabird known for its resilience and tireless wings. But he named me Hai Yen, a pretty name for a girl, because a day before I was born, a swallow flew into our house and built a nest in a ceiling corner. Father said that was a good omen.

I was born mute. I'm sixteen today, Friday. It's my birthday. That means I have to stay in our family's herbal store to help Mother do inventory of the herbal goods, which arrive every Friday. My grandparents own the store. Grandpa is an ethnic Chinese who married Grandma, a southern Vietnamese girl from Ca Mau. Grandpa is like a town doctor who practices the art of therapy to harmonize the *yin* and *yang* in the human body, so that the flow of *qi*, life energy, can be unblocked. Grandpa has a room in the back of the store, where he receives his patients. Mother manages the daily chores in the store, and I help after school. Above Grandpa's rear room is the attic, which has been converted to storage. It has a drop-down ladder. Up in that storage room, stuffy and smelling of dry herbs, Father used to spend his days working on his art. He worked every day after he married Mother. He was fifty-one years old, and Mother was only twenty-five. He'd known her since she was ten. At that time, he was still on the other side, a communist propagandist, who occasionally slipped into Ông Doc town to buy herbal medicines at our family's store and would sometimes receive acupuncture from Grandpa. They became friends; Grandpa was ten years older than Father. Then, a few years before 1975, Father defected to our side, the Republic of Vietnam.

In 1975, when South Vietnam fell to communism, Father disappeared. For ten years. Then one day, he came into our store, gaunt and wearing threadbare clothes, his familiar, long black hair now completely gray. Shortly after, he married Mother. In fact, she'd a teenage crush on him, a man old enough to be her father. Two years later, in 1987, I was born.

I've grown up in our family home, which sits within three kilometers of the town limits. Grandma takes care of the house and the cooking. She raises me and has become my surrogate mother. I didn't see much of Father. Occasionally he'd take me to places I'd never seen, and the people he met usually didn't pay me, a mute, much attention. But Father and I shared a bond that brought us together, a spoken silence. We could feel each other's thoughts, since Father rarely spoke.

When I turned seven, Father made a trip to North Vietnam. He told Mother he wanted to revisit his birthplace, which he hadn't seen in forty years. The year was 1994.

Father never came back. The grown-ups at home would whisper among themselves when they talked about him. I asked them why Father didn't come back. Grandpa, Grandma, and Mother all said, "He belongs to where he is." I could never figure out what that meant, but the line soon became a mantra in our household. Eventually, I stopped asking.

Six months before I turned sixteen, a telegram came. Father was very ill and wished to see both Mother and me. Mother didn't go; she was resolute about it. So, I went alone. She entrusted me to a flight attendant on the plane, who thought I was an adult because of my height.

I stayed in a stilt house on a hillside that overlooked a creek flowing through a ravine. Father had lived in that house in the valley. There were many hills and creeks in that valley, which is called Dien Bien Phu and sits in a remote northwestern region of North Vietnam. Father told me he had nothing valuable to give me, his only daughter, except his diary, artwork. He gave me a suitcase in which he kept his new work and a journal he'd kept since he'd returned to Dien Bien Phu. But the bulk of his work is kept in a trunk in the attic of our family herbal store.

He'd lived there for years, his second home, among jars of redolent medicinal herbs and cartoned herbs that made your skin tingle. Over his years as North Vietnamese propagandist, Father had sought ways to safeguard his works, and he'd found a haven for them in the attic of Grandpa's herbal store.

On the last day of his life, Father asked me if I remembered the story he'd told me when I was seven—how my name came about. I signed to him that the swallow is a good omen when it flies into a home. Father smiled a rare smile. He spoke with his eyes closed, and I leaned into his face to hear the words. He said I was the caretaker of his works and that was my inheritance. I made a sign that I understood. I was—am—the good omen.

Floating Market

The floating market on Ông Doc River runs through our town. Father took me there once when I was six. He carried me in his arms, and we stood on a bridge, looking down. I could see rows of boats and sampans moored along the riverbank, and the water was silvery in the morning sun. Nobody knows how or when the floating market came into being. Perhaps when some sampans came to rest along the sleepy bank, the oarswomen asked each other for a light—maybe a betel chew, a bottle gourd, a pumpkin, or a dash of nuoc mam, fish sauce. And, after a while, a little flea market took to life, and then, one day, a floating market was born.

He didn't buy anything that morning. We stood on the bridge as the sun rose and the river shone white in the mist, which hung like a translucent mosquito net over the sampans. The sleepy river woke at the first sounds of oars as skiffs glided about, thin as a leaf, bringing the first customers to the market. Father carried me down to the bank and asked if I wanted breakfast. The rich aroma of egg pastries wafted up from the bank. I signed with my hand, and Father bought me a wedge of sponge cake that looked like a sea sponge. A woman vendor's voice called out her specialty over the tranquil river. Long bamboo rods rose from the bows of many of the sampans and arched over the water; dangling on the rods was the house's specialty—the ripe, red, hairy rambutans, yellow-tinted papayas, lime-green guavas, deep purple aubergines.

There used to be a boater who was here among all the boater merchants and who sold nothing but one product.

Human merchandise.

She sat that day in the domed shelter hidden behind an all-black curtain hung across the entrance. You could have a peek at her and, if pleased, sit down and play a game of Chinese chess against the boat owner. His daughter, he would tell you, was sixteen. Sunlight bothered her, so the boat's dome was covered with dark drapes. River sounds frayed her nerves, so she always had her ears plugged with cotton. She must be pretty, for men of all ages accepted the invitation for a game of chess, and all left, losing money to the man.

The last time I saw that boatman at the floating market was a week before I traveled to Dien Bien Phu earlier this year. But the first time we were on his boat was the year Father left us, when I was seven. That day, Father decided to play a game of chess against the man. He didn't peek into the dome; he just sat down and played. There was a small crowd that gathered in sampans alongside the man's boat and watched in silence. Some of them were chess players, and others were curiosity seekers. When the morning mist finally lifted hours later, the match was over. On the wooden board, nicked in several places, there were only a few chess pieces left. Father had checkmated the man.

He didn't bother to get to know his prize intimately. He simply shook the man's hand while the crowd looked on in awe. Later, Father told me that during his ten years in the communist reeducation camp, he had learned how to play Chinese chess and played every night before regimented bedtime—and then played on when the oil lamps had been put out by covering the chessboard with a thin blanket and lighting the board with a flicker of a cigarette lighter for each move.

Father must have a deep affection for the floating market, because it was something dear to the natives that we, the Communist northerners, had come to destroy.

The Rainbow Headband

Last night when I was soaking my feet before bedtime, Grandma came in with chunks of alum that looked like ice cubes in her hand. The alum chunks frothed when Grandma dropped them into the pan of warm water. Sometimes Grandma would add a sliver of cinnamon, and it gave the water an acrid scent. I signaled that I felt clean, the soles of my feet tingling and the tingling going up my calves, and Grandma wiped my feet dry with a towel and said, "Little one, you have the most beautiful feet." I sensed then that I must keep my body pure and clean, and I never forget the scent of cinnamon.

Grandma told me that Grandpa's grandmother, who was Chinese and living in China, had her feet bound. I asked what that was, pointing to my own feet. Grandma explained, and I asked her how a girl whose feet were arch-shaped and small from binding could walk. Grandma stepped back and forth, and I laughed. She said it would be a horror to her if my feet were bound.

Last night after soaking my feet, I lay in bed, and sleep wasn't coming. I felt warm in my feet; I brought my hand down to touch them. I pulled up the legs of my pajama pants and looked at my legs and the arc of my full calves, white in the reflected streetlight. I looked down at my chest and knew why Grandma made me wear a brassiere when I went outside. I became more conscious of my full bosom the day I found out from my classmate how she got her rainbow headband. She wasn't as tall as me, and she was flat-chested, yet I envied her for her eyebrows. They arched over her eyes like ink brushstrokes.

She said to me, "You like my headband? See the sequins?"

"It's pretty," I said.

"I got it for free."

"How?"

There was this middle-aged man, she told me, who had a boat and would come into town once a week. He would dock his boat in a cove, and the clinking chime he hung on his boat would tell you he was there with all kinds of trinkets. She went in there, and after looking around she saw a sequin-adorned headband.

"Isn't it pretty on ya?" the man said in his purring voice.

She turned it in her hand, biting her lower lip, and nodded.

"How much money ya got?"

"I don't have money."

He scratched under his chin. "Get some money. I can't keep it for ya."

Reluctantly, she handed the headband back to the man. He raised his eyes from where he sat on the floor. "You really like it, eh?"

She nodded, feeling like a mouse under his stare.

"Keep it." He shrugged as she peered at him. "If you feel bad taking it, do somethin' for me." He pointed at her chest, coughed, spat, and made a sign of unbuttoning her blouse.

I've thought a lot about what she told me. When he saw her breasts, he said, "Come back next time and I'll give you a nice bra. Lacy stuff. Pretty on your nice skin."

She said to me, "Do you want to come with me next time?" She eyed my chest, and I could see a glint of envy in her eyes.

I never considered her invitation. It was vulgar of her. I want to keep my body pure and clean, because I remember how much care Grandma gave it.

First Time

On every Friday I didn't have to stay in our herbal store to take inventory of the herbal goods arriving in the afternoon, Mother would let me go with Grandma to deliver medicine to some folks out of town. These folks showed their gratitude for what cured their illnesses by giving Grandma a laughingthrush in a bamboo-slat cage. It was a cute, black-chinned thrush. Grandma said it could mimic the sounds it heard.

I sat holding the cage in my lap as we went downriver in a boat. A wind chime rang melodiously from another boat going upriver. For a moment, I thought of the man who sold sundries from his boat and the tortoiseshell hair clasp. The laughingthrush puffed its gray-colored breast and sang, pee-koo-pee-koo. Then it blinked its round, honey-brown eyes.

It gazed toward a stand of black mangrove on the shallow edge of the riverbank, where curtainlike roots hung from the tree trunks and touched the water. Those roots nurture oysters and snails that attach to them; that's what Grandma explained, as she always does on our outings. She said pelicans and sometimes parrots or spoonbills shelter in the trees.

A kingfisher shot out of the foliage. The laughingthrush cocked its head, its white-browed eyes gazing after the kingfisher's flight.

I patted Grandma as she braced herself against a sudden lurch. The boat was crossing a river mouth where a stream ran into it, swelling the current.

She looked back at me. "What, dear?"

I signed and pointed to the caged bird, and Grandma said a bird could survive in the wild if set free, but only an adult bird. A baby bird that grew up in a cage would likely die in nature. She asked me why I wanted to set it free, and I thought of the way the bird's eyes had fixed on the kingfisher, as if mesmerized. I signed again and Grandma said, "Let me think about it when we get home."

The boat came alongside a merchant boat, like those I had

seen at the floating market. Shelved inside its dome were rows of candies and preserved fruits in jars, and in the bow were laid-out rattan sieves with orange sesame balls, deep-fried and glistening; steamed bánh bò, pocked-skinned sponge cakes tinted green; and molasses-brown leaf-jelly cubes in plastic cups. Grandma bought a big jar of golden sugar that gleamed like sand. She said it was made from sugarcane.

As our boat moved again, past the merchant boat's stern, I saw a young girl washing herself. She didn't see me. Skinny and long-haired, she looked younger than me. Her skin was pale white in the sun as she squatted in the stern over a pail of water, her floral-pink pantaloons pushed down to her ankles as she washed her crotch with her hand. The water was tinged red.

The first time I had bled like that, I was thirteen. I thought something evil had entered my body, and I got under a blanket and cried. Grandma said, "Nothing's wrong, dear. It's normal for girls."

The Leper Isle

Once, when I was seven, I went in a boat with Father to Leper Isle. It sat like a dark swell in the middle of the fast-flowing Ông Doc River. Father said a century ago, the lepers made the isle their home. The ostracized caste fended for themselves in their refuge, and, over the years, many of them had died from drowning when they took to the water.

Father didn't tell me why he went there with me on that day. Years later, I learned from Grandma that the isle used to be a Viet Cong haven during the war, a place for them to stash their cache of weapons and ammunition. I imagine when Father was still a North Vietnamese communist, he had been to the Leper Isle. What brought him back there, I don't know. Perhaps memories.

That same year, Father left us to return to the North. He never came back. Sometime after that, a intellectual disability woman from our town was found dead on the bank of Leper Isle, her body snagged on the stilt roots of crabapple mangrove. She was in her thirties, often trailed by mischievous children on the streets, whom she would chase off when they started throwing rocks at her. The year before, she had gotten pregnant. Some river man must have lured her onto his boat, a fisherman or a sundries boat merchant. Or a shopkeeper in town who gave her a floral blouse and said its plum-colored fabric went nicely with her milky-white skin.

And she was blessed with such fine skin. Sometimes, she would casually squat on a sidewalk, push her satiny black pantaloons past her thighs, and urinate with passersby moving up and down the sidewalk, many of them pretending not to look—but those who peeped were men, salivating at the smooth white of her buttocks. During her pregnancy, I saw her grab any man who came within her reach. "You dirty goat," she said shrilly. "I've been looking for you. You made my belly swell up like this and you pull up your pants and scoot away." And the men would cringe, then jerk away, some cursing, some red in the face.

She liked to bathe at night and left her clothes on deadwood carried to the riverbank by high tides. Some rascals would hide her clothes and then watch her cavorting in the water, cursing and calling out the names of their ancestors, three generations deep. When they recovered her body on Leper Isle, they speculated that she must have drowned—or worse, been raped by those bargemen who often went downriver late at night.

Then the stories went around that the half-wit woman sometimes came up at night on the riverbank, sitting without clothes on a rock facing Leper Isle, waiting for any man to come and copulate with her. I don't know how much of it was true. But something about the woman stayed with me. Perhaps it was that she was born with no intelligence and I without the capability of speech.

One day, I asked Grandma why a person is born with a handicap while others are normal. Grandma took a moment to think, then pulled me into her and said, "It's your karma.

Pay for it in full before you become normal again."

The Sundry Boat

One day last week, Grandma and I rode home in an oxcart. We were the only two passengers, and our cart was pulled by a big, black bull. As we were leaving the open-air market, there was a woman leading a fawn-colored cow by the halter ahead of us. The bull suddenly sprang, lifting its forelegs off the ground, and charged after the cow. It jumped over the cow's rear end with the harness on its back, the collar around its neck, the wooden shafts of the cart on its sides, and pitched the cart up on a tilt, slamming its rear against the ground.

We slid back. Grandma screamed. Her head bounced as it hit the slatted side of the cart. The old man driving the cart lashed the bull with a whip, jerking it back on the reins. He cursed and shouted as he yanked on the reins until the bull relented and dismounted. The woman pulled her cow away, but only after shaking her finger at the old man.

"Get that horny bull castrated," she said. "Cut his things off!"

Grandma found her tortoiseshell barrette on the ground just as the cart moved back, the bull still snorting and trampling the ground back and forth, and the wheel went over the barrette. I could hear it snap. So, Grandma berated the old man, and he apologized to her until she calmed down and told him to get moving again. She was sore because that tortoiseshell barrette has been with her before I was even born.

I thought of buying Grandma another hair pin and then forgot. Earlier this week, I was walking home from an errand by taking the riverbank, and as I walked past rows of boats being docked at rest, I heard a wind chime. It hung outside the curved dome of a sundry boat moored against the wharf; one of the boat's sides was clad with several tires. The breeze swung the black wooden turtle that swam above stringed bamboo tubes in ivory yellow. The tubes clanged with colored glass beads dangling among them, and they made mellow sounds in the breeze.

I hesitated before stepping onto the boat's deck. I liked the barrette my classmate got on this boat. It wasn't as nice as Grandma's old barrette, but maybe I could find another one just as pretty. When I bent low to enter the domed shelter, I saw the man and thought of how my classmate got her sequined headband from him, and I almost stepped back out.

He grinned at me from where he sat on a low stool. His tobacco-stained teeth were uneven, and some were sharp like a dog's. He was holding a jar shaped like a garlic head when I entered. Slowly, he uncorked the jar. The cork was made of a dried banana leaf twisted and tied with its fibers. I was wearing a knee-length black skirt and a short-sleeved white shirt, and my hair kept falling across my face as I bent to find my footing. I could smell fermented rice, perhaps from what he drank in that jar. He took a sip from the jar, and his eyes screwed to slits, taking me in.

"Anything in particular I can get f'ya?" he said in a phlegmy voice.

I panicked. I don't interact much with people, except when I stay in Grandpa's herbal store to help Mother out. So, I made hand signs to tell him what I wanted.

His eyes opened wide. "Ya can't speak, huh? Can ya hear?" I nodded.

"Ah, poor thin'." He gestured, his hand still clutching the jar. "Look 'round. Plenty of girlie thin's f'a pretty girl like ya. Look 'round."

I wasn't going to stay any longer than I had to.

He nodded, his nicotine-darkened lips pursed. "Have all sorts of girlie thin's f'hair. In those containers, honey. Knickknacks. Them thin's look pretty on ya. Necklaces, bracelets, lockets, earrings. Got a mermaid hair comb and all kinds of hair pins. Just look 'round, pretty youn' thin'."

There were shelves nailed to wooden curved slats that supported the dome, and on the shelves were glass jars and plastic containers, big and small, and hanging from the domed ceiling were knickknacks, like brass jewelry, wood-carved animals—a deer head, a painted beetle—and blown glass ornaments. They jingled when a breeze blew in, and when my head touched a glass egg, I stopped moving. I turned to those clear plastic containers on the shelves.

The man groped his way to the stern. I picked up a brass necklace that had a little girl on a swing. I put it on my chest, where my shirt opened into a V at the top. The metal felt cold against my skin. I put it back and picked up a pair of earrings. They gleamed silvery-white with two little birds, each with a little leaf dangling below. I don't have my ears pierced, but my classmate does, the one who got the hair headband from the owner of this boat. She wore crescent-moon earrings made of bone of some kind, bone-white and pretty.

I saw the mermaid hair comb. It was bronze and had a glass cabochon set in the center with a picture of a sitting mermaid in it. I really liked it, so I didn't put it back. In a next container there were hair claws with blue or brown marbled grips, and hair clips with a brass butterfly inset with colored glass stones. They looked too youthful for Grandma. Then, at the bottom of the container, I saw a tortoiseshell hair claw that looked like a rusty-red centipede with golden claws. It was pretty and simple, just like Grandma.

As I held it in one hand with the mermaid comb in the other hand, I felt the boat moving. I bent lower to peer out of the domed shelter and saw the boat was now midstream, the wharf smaller in the distance. I saw the man grope his way back in, bent, both hands on the floor like a simian. He rose slowly, still half-crouched, until his head touched a dangling tassel necklace.

He gripped me by the wrists and brought my hands against his face. "Ya like 'em?" He sniffed my hands. "Ya smell so nicey. Lemme give ya somethin' worth wearin'." And he lifted the brass necklace that had the little girl on a swing and said, "Wear it. I have it in black glass, too, and aya, that color is pretty on y' youn'un."

He smelled bad. I backed away. The sight of the distant wharf alarmed me. I made a panicked sound, but it came out like a whine. He said, "I wish ya could speak, 'cause ya must got a sweet voice—come, come, lemme put it on ya, youn' thin'." He fumbled with the top button of my shirt. I pushed his hands away. He yanked down on it. The button snapped, and, for one second, he seemed frozen as he stared at my chest and moaned, "Ah, ya angel—ya skin—ya a beautiful youn' thin'." He pulled me down, his grubby face already buried in my chest. "Ah, ya smell so nicey—lemme smell yah sweet lil' pot—now, now—doncha be scared—"

He pulled me down, and I felt his rough hand go up my skirt. I clamped my legs and hit his face with the mermaid comb. The comb's teeth raked across his stubbled face. He fell back, touching his eyes, and I stumbled out of the dome, my head hitting the dangling ornaments. They clanked. I waved frantically at a boat coming downriver toward us, screaming, but the sound that left my throat was garbled.

He grabbed my hair and yanked me back. I swung around, my shirt flying, and felt the breeze on my chest. He dragged me back in. I hit him with my fist, the mermaid comb breaking against his head, and I hit him again with the other hand and broke the tortoiseshell hair pin too. He threw me down on the floor, his legs bent, planted on both sides of me, and leered down at me. "Ya have a notion of what ya did?" A corner of his upper lip raised, showing his yellowed canine tooth. "Ya ain't gonna rob me of what I want, not in did worl', naw naw—" He flung up the bottom of my skirt just as the boat shook. I brought my hands down there, panting, nearly in tears, and he grabbed both my hands by the wrists and made a strange guttural sound in his throat as he cut his eyes at my lower body.

That was when I saw a woman at the dome entrance, bent low, peering in. I knew her. The old woman who owned a riverboat. Grandma and I had ferried in her boat when Grandma had to go to Leper Isle to buy herbal pots.

The man snapped his head back to see the old woman crouching over him, holding a long oar in her hand.

"You dirty old goat," she said, baring her teeth,

red-stained from betel chew.

He rose gingerly, and as he did, I slid away from him and stood. My head hit the ceiling, and the brass trinkets tinkled. The woman gestured at me with her hand. "Go out to the stern, dear thing. My boat is there."

The man neither looked at me nor the old woman. He just remained in one spot, slouched.

I got off the sundry boat.

As the old woman rowed her boat toward the wharf, she cast a curious glance at me. "You don't need to tell me anything, dear little one. I can't understand you anyway. You can tell your grandma, though. Maybe someone can do something about it." She kept rowing as I tucked in my shirt in and sat, pinching the top of it with my fingers. I felt grateful to her, but I couldn't speak.

Like the sundry boat's owner, the old woman drank, too. When she ferried us to Leper Isle, she would wait for Grandma and sometimes me in her boat, and I'd doze while waiting and wake up to the yeasty, faintly sweet smell of rice wine and see her sitting on a reed mat toward the stern, a glass jar being warmed on a brazier. Sometimes, Grandma would share a cup of rice wine with her on the back.

Along the riverway to Leper Isle, mangrove groves rose from tangled roots on the muddy bank, forming a tall stand to bear the storms coming in from the sea. Mangrove logs would pave the steps that led to riverside shanties, and sometimes, as the boat passed by, I would see mudskippers carried in by the tide, walking on their fins, flicking their goggled eyes around. Leper Isle was near the sea, and between the shanties you could see huge fishnets hanging on poles. Sometimes, the stench of fish would follow you downwind; other times, a yeasty wind-borne smell followed the boat. The old woman said it came from homemade brew, where broken rice was fermented and distilled.

Since I was seven, around the time Father went back to the North, Grandma has gone to Leper Isle to buy ceramic pots, and she's always ferried downriver in the old woman's boat. Once I asked Grandma what was so special about those ceramic pots that she had to go there to buy them for Grandpa. She said a century ago, it was a haven for the lepers, until one day a band of brigands came and built their own sanctuary with the lepers' labor. When it was completed, the bandits herded all the lepers to a pit and burned them, and afterward, they dumped lime on the charred remains and filled the pit. The local government caught wind of the massacre and brought in its naval fleet to lay siege to the isle. After several weeks, the bandits ran out of food and began killing one another. Those who came out to surrender were hung along the shore until shore birds and vultures pecked their flesh away. In the end, the government troops moved in and buried every bandit alive in a pit next to the mass burial ground of the lepers, under the district chief's order.

Then, after the war ended in 1975, an entrepreneur built a kiln on the isle. The hard clay came from the old burial sites. Once fired to 1200 degrees Celsius, the clay came out oxblood-red. The ceramic pots they made were glazed dark red, clear sounding when you tapped it with your fingernails, and bounced off the cement floor when dropped. Grandpa cooked his herbs only in the clay pots made on Leper Isle, then stocked and sold them to his clients.

When we reached the wharf, the old woman shipped the oar and looked at me, still clutching the top of my shirt. "Listen, dear little one. You're pretty and smart. But there are people who think a disabled person is something like an imbecile. A deaf, a mute—their misconception brings out the predator in them, like that lewd old goat. But you shouldn't be ashamed of what you are. Just be more careful when you deal with people. You hear?"

I nodded. I wished to thank her, but I knew she wouldn't understand my language. I walked home, pinning the top of my shirt with my hand. I thought of the tortoiseshell hair clasp, the color of a rusty-red centipede, and I didn't know if I should tell Grandma about what happened to me.

A Scent of Long-Ago Love

The Opium Den

The first time my employer took me to an opium den on Cholon, the old Chinatown in Saigon, he rode in one pedicab and I in the other, following him, carrying his trinkets in a round wicker basket—his pipe, a teapot, two tiny handleless cups, and sugary confections wrapped inside two layers of brown paper.

The door opened into a narrow, dimly lit hall by the red glow of the lamps. A sweet caramel odor, warm and intoxicating. I stared into the murkiness. Small peanut oil lamps flickered in their crystal globes, illuminating half-naked bodies that lay on mats, propping themselves on cushions. My employer stepped carefully between the mats, saying not a word, and I kept close to him as we picked our way past the burning lamps that sent smoky spirals to the ceiling. At the end of the hall, there was a bead curtain that clanked when one went through it. The world behind it glowed in a soft light from the paper lanterns, round and yellow, that hung from the rafters. Silk parasols in guava green, aqua blue, and bright lilac leaned in the gossamer light at the heads of narrow, low-lying beds of carved wood. Bodies reclined in eddying plumes, the opium crackling over low-necked lamps. My employer told me to tend my tasks as quietly as a mouse, never talk to the servants, and never to stare at the patrons while they were deep in their reveries.

I was in awe the first time I set foot inside the den. After my employer lay down on a low bed made of wood, I sat gingerly on the edge of it. Its fine curved legs were carved with pale, glittering mother-of-pearl etchings of small tortoises and cranes and dwarfed trees. I touched the dark red satin sheet. It was cool, smooth. After a while, I looked up at the yellow silk canopy dangling with tassels above me. The room flickered with peanut oil lamps, their crystal globes a handsome bulbous shape, and they suddenly grew dim when a patron leaned out, drawing deeply on his pipe. Over the door hung an orange paper lantern attached to the ceiling. When I gazed up at the beautiful tear-shape, still and solitary, I thought of an ethereal world free of all pain, all worries. I breathed in a dark odor of caramel, and the room came to life with the occasional crackling of pipes.

I didn't know opium smelled like burnt sugar. My employer explained that only premium opium smelled that way. He said base opium had an unpleasant smell.

He was very picky about his opium habit. He didn't like the tea served by the den's servants, so he had me brew it just as he began preparing his first pipe. The tea must be hot when he drank it. That was why the teapot held just a pinch of his select tea, enough to make two tiny cups. I had to brew it again and again. Three months after I went to work for him, he taught me how to prepare a pipe. Reclining on his elbow, he watched me.

I heated a wooden-handled needle over the lamp and dipped it into the crystal opium jar, watching the brown drug glue itself to the tip of the pin. I could sense his following my every move as I brought the needle to the lamp and cooked the sticky drop. I twirled the pin, the lamp burning a soft yellow. I watched the drop intently, and then it swelled, glistening a brown color. I picked it off the pin and kneaded it against the palm of my hand until it became puttylike. Then, holding my breath, I pushed the paste neatly into the tiny opening of the bowl. With both hands, I held the pipe over the lamp, ignoring the heat on my fingertips, and watched the dark brown opium melt into smoke. He brought his lips to the stem and drew in the smoke as deeply as he could. His eyes slowly closed, his head tilted back, and then he exhaled the smoke through his nostrils and mouth. I kept the pipe still as his lips again found the pipe stem and his cheeks hollowed as he sucked in the fumes.

He would take five draws before preparing a fresh pipe. Some evenings, he smoked fifteen pipes, some evenings twenty. Between drags, he sipped tea and nibbled a caramel confection, savoring the taste as it melted in his mouth. His wife made delectable sweetmeats. Then he napped. I started cleaning his pipe. One of the items in the basket I carried was a thin iron pin that I used to scrape out the opium dregs in the blowhole of the pipe bowl.

In the opposite corner of the room stood a canary-yellow silk screen framed in shiny black wood. Behind the silk screen, you could glimpse the girls changing their attire before they came out to entertain the patrons. They would come out dressed in shiny green or blue or red moiré cheongsams. When one of them came to my employer's bed, I could sometimes smell a lemon or rose scent when she slid in at his side. Her smooth, white skin made his skin look sickly and pale in comparison, and when she reached for the pipe, her dress was pulled back tight, and I could see the whiteness of her upper arms where the sleeves stopped a finger-length short of her armpits. I couldn't take my eyes from her blood-red fingernails.

Before I came, my employer had to do all these chores by himself—he had to prepare his pipe and brew his own tea, not to mention carry all his playthings himself. Now he had me, a college student who worked as his attendant on nights he needed me and who earned a pittance to help pay his own lodging and food. My employer smoked up to twenty pipes in a night. One night while he napped, I was cleaning his pipe, and a den servant came to me and asked me to let him have the dregs I was scraping out of the pipe's bowl. I looked up at him and then at a piece of brown paper he held in his hand.

"Why?" I asked. "I'll trash this myself."

"Just give it to me."

"You sell them?"

"Yeah."

"Who buys?"

"Street drug addicts."

"They smoke this crap?"

"Yeah. Smoke. Drink. Mix it with tobacco. Tonic for them."

"And good money for you."

"A sin to waste even crap."

From that night on, I thought of saving up the opium residues and selling them to the addicts. But where would I find the dope fiends? And how many visits to the den with my employer would it take for me to earn money? Each patron, I noticed, smoked fifteen to thirty pipes an evening. Even a light smoker could go for ten pipes before he nodded off. If I cleaned every pipe in the den, how much could I earn selling this sort of poison?

The Soot-Faced Girl

One evening as we were leaving the den, a drizzle was falling. As always, my employer would carry his opium basket back while riding in a pedicab, and I would walk home.

The air smelled fresh as a cool breeze was coming from the river. I turned onto a crossroad that ran perpendicular to the river. Two human figures moved across the street in the wavering reflection of a lantern. They were barefoot and seemed to glide in darkness. A child, clothed in rags, pulled a blind old man along with one hand, holding in his other hand a red paper lantern at the end of a stick. I watched the child and the blind man heading into a wild banana grove by the roadside. The red of their lantern dimmed, wavering eerily, and suddenly disappeared. Then in the blackness of the grove a torch light glowed.

A group of men, at least ten, squatted around the torch. They were Chinese. You could see their shaved heads. They were haggling over something from the harsh sounds they made. Finally, they stood up, each looking at something in his hands. Standing in the center was a girl counting coins. They clanked as she dropped them into her bag. Her soot-covered face, so black in the dancing torch light, looked ghoulish. Was she hiding her face so she could go unnoticed while peddling the illegal drug? I wondered. She swung her bag over her shoulder, her plait dangling behind her, and strode out of the grove.

Suddenly, out of the darkness a motorcyclist rode up. He rode up so quickly that everyone, including me, just stared at him, bewildered, for a moment. A drug trafficking cop. Perhaps he had been there, waiting in the dark, unseen, for his whole outfit was black. He wore a tight-looking leather jacket and trousers that were tucked into his black boots. Even his motorcycle was black as an otter. He shouted something in Vietnamese, and the Chinese broke off running out of the grove. The torch remained on the ground, sputtering with blue sparks. The girl froze. I touched my knife I had tucked under my belt. Where the hilt met the sheath's opening, it was banded with a metal clasp that had a small ring. I had run a short string through it.

The cop strode over to the edge of the grove. Before she could even move, he reached into her bag and pulled something out. A bad feeling hit me. She must be selling opium dregs. He kicked the torch over, dragged her to his motorbike by her braid, and swung himself back up on the seat. He coasted along, the girl being dragged by her braid alongside, tumbling over her feet as her arms flailed. I didn't know what to do. Then I ran after them. I stumbled on something, and I dropped to the ground. A rock. I picked it up and stood, sucking in my pain. I let it fly. The motorcycle veered; the black shape dropped to the ground. The girl tottered. I ran up to her. Fright burned my dry throat. Had I just killed a cop?

"Run!" I shouted to her.

We squeezed through the grove and then came back out on the streets. My ears buzzed; my breathing came in gasps.

In a dark alley, she stopped running and slumped against a wall. Gasping, I walked up to her. Her face was so dark only her white teeth showed in the black alley.

"What's your name?" I asked in Vietnamese.

She was silent and simply looked at me. Then she said, "Xiaoli."

She was Chinese. "Did he ever get you before, that drug cop?"

"The policeman?" she said in a slight accent. "You killed him, yes?"

"I hope not," I said, pained. Then I spoke slowly to her, "What you did is very dangerous."

"Don't I know that?"

"Then why keep doing it?"

"Why are you asking?"

I shook my head. To her, I was a stranger who happened to save her. "You work in an opium den?"

"Yes."

"Where?"

"You will come?"

"I don't smoke opium."

She thought for a moment and then spoke. Her hands drew invisible directions. I heard the name Sail Street, then a cross street somewhere that had no name, but where there was an old woman on the corner selling silk from early morning till dusk. Off the cross street was an alley with shops and houses. The den had no name.

"Ask for me if you are lost," she said.

"Ask? Who?" I asked.

"The silk woman. She doesn't talk. She knows me."

"Ask for Xiaoli?"

"No. They call me White Lily."

"She understands? Say White Lily in Chinese."

She said it slowly and swung her cloth bag onto her back. "I must get on home."

"I'll walk with you," I said.

"This way." She pointed in the direction of the street we

were heading toward. Even blackened with soot, her face was gentle, with soft lines flowing from her well-shaped nose to her lips and chin.

A cross street up beyond the alley entrance. A pedicab went past. A cart squeaked by on four little wheels. A man was pushing it up the street, and on one side of the cart hung a lantern. The side was painted with red Chinese characters. I couldn't tell what they said. Perhaps they told of his trade. I could see a pair of ducks, brown with fire and glinting with grease, hung upside down on a rod. Past a corner, an odor of late-night noodles came drifting, and with it came the odor of opium. Squalid dens were squeezed into those dark alleys.

She turned into an alley. Shards of a broken vat lay strewn across the dirt. They crunched under my shoes. The alley dead-ended with a wall—set in it was a red door framed with wrought iron.

"I live here," she said. "I'm a maid."

"Here—and in the opium den?"

"Yes."

"You sneak out at night—to go to the den?"

"What?"

"They let you out? The family you work for."

"They own the den."

She opened the big door with a bulky key and then dropped it back in the bag. It clanked against the coins. She turned to me. "Would you like to sit in the garden?"

"I would love that," I said.

There was a wood bench by a rockwork basin. I sat there and waited for her. She disappeared into the house through a side door that had a small, round mirror above the doorway. Later, she would tell me that a mirror over a door guarded against malign spirits. The full moon washed the blue tiled roofs with yellow light. The quiet made my heart throb with an unknown trepidation. She came out soundlessly like a cat. She had a tin can in her hand, and her face was clean of black soot. I couldn't help but gaze at her face. Her pupils were black, her eyes so symmetrically shaped and clear that I felt thick in my throat.

"I sit here every night when there is a full moon," she said as she sat down beside me. "I want to see if the silver carp will come up."

I looked toward the rock basin where she pointed.

"What silver carp?" I asked.

"It lives in there," she said, flicking her gaze toward the basin. "If you are the one who sees it jump from the water when the full moon is just above it, something wonderful will happen to you."

She sipped from the tin can and then handed it to me. I drank. Cold and fragrant and sweet. I shivered. She said it was *hong cha*. I knew the tea. My employer drank it. She said she added some white sugar and lemon and left it in a thick clay pot in the cellar where they kept fresh herbs and vegetables for the household. I peered up at the sky. In its dead blackness, the moon hung so bright its halo was a shade paler.

She drew a sharp breath. "Such a beautiful sight!"

A shadow crossed the dark garden. We watched a cat saunter off the brick walk into the darkness, its eyes two shining marbles.

"Watch the night sky," she said. "Sometimes you see a falling star. It might tell you someone close to you just died." She paused, then said, "If it falls in the direction where someone you know lives."

I handed her the tin can. "You ever seen one?"

"Yes."

"Where did it fall to?"

"North. My home."

"China?"

"Yes."

"How long ago?"

"Months ago."

"But many people live there. What're the odds?"

"But not many people see a falling star."

"What made you think someone you love died when you saw it?"

"I just know. My mother might have died."

A hollow in my stomach seized my breath. "Why?" I asked.

"Mother is very poor and ill."

"And your father?"

"No father. Only Mother."

"Will you ever leave that place?"

"What place?"

"The opium lair."

"When I save enough. I will go back to my mother."

"What's your family name?"

"Zhang." Then she smiled. "You have a name?"

"Tài."

"You don't speak Chinese," she said. "No?"

"No." I could speak a few words that I learned from my employer. But her words made me feel warm again deep down. "When can I see you again?"

"Come to the quay tomorrow night."

The Quay

The following night I went to the quay. The smell of the river was in the air. It was muddy and foul with waste, fish and bamboo scraps, rotten cabbage and orange peels. There were lights on the quay. I stood back under an Indian almond tree. Sampans and junks and small steam ships dotted the water's edge, and the quay lay trembling in the yellowy light of the lanterns. On the gangplank, the coolies stood naked above the waist. Some sat slumped against the rail, and some lay like corpses on top of coiled ropes. I felt my knife.

A sudden smashing sound startled me. One of the coolies rose from the planks, raising his fist. I could see an opium pipe in his clenched hand. He was half naked, his torso ox-blood and his arms sinewy. He kicked the broken neck of a lamp with his bare foot, and it shattered against a wooden pile. The other coolies hollered, jabbing their fingers at him as he brought his other hand up to his mouth. I saw a glinting shard of glass. You could hear him crunch it with his teeth as if he were crunching ice cubes. Then he chewed. His companions laughed and gawked and spat, and the dazed coolie chewed on. There were red threads coming out of his mouth, and you could see him trying to swallow with difficulty. When he finally did, his head jerked and the other coolies' bantering suddenly subsided.

Then, I saw her.

Out of darkness she emerged, lithe, quick-stepping, a cloth bag flung across her shoulder, her braid bouncing. She moved swiftly onto the quay. Like ants to sugar, they swarmed around her. The stuporous coolie stood mumbling to himself. I caught a glimpse of her blackened face between thrusting arms and snatching hands. The coins clanked. I hurried out to the quay, my eyes fixed on the disturbed coolie.

He tucked his pipe into his trousers, bent, picked up another broken piece of glass, and fed it into his mouth. He crunched it, chewed. Then he stopped. His arms flailed. Blood was coming out the corners of his mouth as he teetered toward a lantern. All the coolies were oblivious to him before he came crashing into them. He flung his arm and grabbed her by the shoulder. The other coolies cursed and shoved him back, and coins fell clanking. I grabbed him by the arm that held her. His arm was hard. He yanked her toward him, and she fell smack against his chest. The coolies broke up. He had his hand in her bag as I pummeled his face. His head didn't even move. All I saw were the slits of his eyes, his bulging teeth, and a shaven head, pale to the top. I saw a knife in his hand. He grabbed her by the neck as though he was angered she had kept him waiting. I pulled out my knife. She was flailing her arms in his grip. I moved in just as his knife came at my stomach.

I grabbed the blade. My knees locked, my hand screamed with pain, and I felt him seize me by the back of my neck. I was helpless as his knife went into my body. My breath was cut off. The only thing that kept me standing was my will: *Don't die!* My head hit his shoulder, and I willed my hand that clutched the knife to drive it up into his chest. I grunted. Something was forced up from my convulsed stomach, and I tasted blood.

He fell, and my knife became dislodged from his chest. Lying on my back, I saw a black sky, and I could taste more blood in my mouth now, and I gagged, trying to breathe. She squatted down beside me, her eyes searching my face as if she wanted an answer. Then she saw my cut hand cupping my stomach. The handle of his knife protruded outside my body. I saw her looking down, a face black as the sky above. Then she cried. Footfalls. Faces. The shaved heads. The gray blouses. Like they all came together in the same picture. She cried hysterically. She shouted in Chinese, and the Chinese coolies, frenzied, yelled among themselves. Someone ran out to the street with a torch. She dropped her gaze to my hand that still clutched my own knife, unclasped my fingers, and then tried to sheathe it. After she secured it under my belt, she cupped her hand over mine on my stomach. Her other hand wiped the blood that had started leaking from the corner of my mouth. I couldn't see very well because of a wet film over my eyes, and my nose felt soggy. I had to breathe through my mouth. Beneath me the earth shook. I heard the clacking of wheels. She was crying out to someone.

Melody of a Bygone Past

For one moment before coming out of a blackness, I heard a soothing, peaceful melody. Across the plank bed, a long bar of sunlight fell from the latticed window high above, where a patch of blue sky hung. This wasn't my place. I could tell. The plank bed was raised on a platform. It had a headrest, a footrest. I was lying on a thin floral quilt. I was alive. I had a body. Its midsection was wrapped heavily in white cloth under a gray shirt put on me. My head rested against a round wooden pillow covered in blue linen. Was I in a room of somebody's home? The melody. Was I hallucinating?

I slept, woke, and slept again. Each time I woke, my

abdomen and my hand twinged. When I moved my body, it hurt. Once I woke, I caught myself groaning. She was sitting on the edge of the bed, holding a clay bowl.

"I brought you medicine," she said.

I looked at her. Her ponytail was flung over her shoulder, touching her abdomen. Her dark blue blouse had a sheen. I tried to find words. She was real, no more a furtive figure gliding through the night. At my silence, she moved the bowl to my lips. I sipped the first taste of liquid and winced. She held the rim of the bowl near my lips, her fingers long and tapered, and I saw the white facings of her sleeves' cuffs. I leaned forward and took another sip, this time holding it in my mouth until the herbal smell stung my nose. I gulped down the warm liquid. She watched me calmly, patiently. I took hold of the bowl and her hands as they held it.

"Let me—" I said and felt a sharp twitch in my left hand. The bowl spilled onto my chest.

Quickly, she wiped it with her hand. "Don't use your hand," she said. "Rest it."

There was something yellow like turmeric on the palm of my cut hand and fingers. The yellow powder had caked on the slashes, but it hurt sharply when I made a fist. I sipped and swallowed with difficulty, and, each time I gazed up, I met her eyes, steadily watching me. For the last sip I took, I had to lean my head back as she tilted the bowl almost upside down, and it covered my face completely.

"Xiaoli," I said, choked, liquid dripping from my lips.

"Oh, I'm clumsy," she said, giggling, then suddenly solemn. "You saved me twice."

I took in her gentle features for one brief moment while she looked down. "How did you end up selling opium?"

"Ah," she said, crimping her lips.

I could see her thick lashes flutter. She seemed to be searching for something to say. Finally, she looked up. "This . . . merchant, yes, merchant, gave my mother some money, loaned money, yes. I was eleven. I went in a ship with many women and little girls like me. They made many of us take opium, so we don't cry while we are at sea . . . ." Now I understood why she was so bent on selling opium dregs to earn extra money: to buy out her bondage because of her mother's debt. I met her gaze. Each time I felt thick in the throat. "Are you hungry?" she asked.

The pain seemed to be the only thing I felt.

She smiled as she rose. "I'll bring you something to eat."

I heard a cuckoo in the quiet. From the latticed window, the streak of sunlight had become longer across the floor. Watching it, I wondered about the time of day. Then I noticed a fresh pair of cotton trousers on me. Mine must have been covered with bloodstains.

I felt hot in the head. Who changed my clothes?

She came back, carrying a small bamboo food steamer. It had two decks, round, veined with gray stains from steam and heat from cooking. She lifted the lid of the top deck. In it there were two white steamed buns.

"I made them," she said, handing me one.

It was warm as I held it in my good hand. Steam was coming from its silky skin. "I eat one," I said. "You eat one."

I chewed. It tasted sweet, with a bamboo fragrance clinging to its skin. I watched her take a bite, forgetting my discomfort. In the quiet we ate.

"I need to wash your wounds later," she said.

"You? Why?"

"The physician said you must change bandages twice a day. Or you might get infection."

I swallowed what was in my mouth and opened my cut hand. "What is this yellow stuff?"

"That? Ah." She squinted her eyes, thought, and said something to herself in Chinese. Then she raised her face at me. "I don't know what it is here, in this country. It's a round fruit like an egg. Its flesh is yellow and thick."

I thought of the mamey sapote. "*Cây trứng gà*," I said.

"That's what it is. They grind the seeds into powder. It heals cuts." She dropped her gaze to my midsection. "You passed out in the pedicab. We didn't know if you would ever wake up again. You lost so much blood you would have died if we had not taken you back to the house in time." At my silence, she continued. "We have a family physician nearby. That's why I avoided taking you to a hospital." She gestured with her hand toward the courtyard. "I washed your clothes. They had much blood on them. I will patch your shirt when it's dried."

"You're very kind, Xiaoli."

"Because of me you almost died."

"Don't say that."

The cuckoo called again. A desolate sound in the quiet.

"I must wash your wound now and dress it," she said.

"Is it afternoon now?" I asked.

She nodded, picked up the steamer, and left the room. She came back shortly with a brass pail of water and a handkerchief, a roll of white cloth draped over her forearm. Without saying a word, she moved up to me and began removing the pins that fastened the strip of cloth around my midsection. She unwrapped it deftly, lifting me up with her hand pressed against the small of my back. I held my breath, watching her hands and then the wound. It was covered with the yellow powder. She wrung the handkerchief and gently washed the powder away. My chest heaved. A faint lemon scent got in my nostrils. It wasn't from the water or the powder. By then I could see the gash, red and raw, and her fingers dabbing it with the fresh yellow powder she took from a pouch in her blouse pocket. When she unrolled the fresh cloth strip, I pushed myself up from the bed with both hands and let her wind the strip around my midsection. Her face was calm as she dressed my wound. She never frowned. Her skin was so clear, her nose straight and so finely shaped. I noticed the nick on her throat. That addict could have killed her had I not killed him.

"Who changed my clothes?" I said quietly.

"Me," she said, glancing quickly at me and dropped her gaze.

I inhaled sharply, but she did not see.

"I will change the bandage again tonight," she said,

buttoning up the side of my blouse.

"How long will I be staying here?"

"Until you are healed." She washed her hands in the pail. "When you can walk again."

"Where's your room?"

"Here."

"This room?"

She nodded and flung her ponytail back over her shoulder.

"I can sleep anywhere else but here," I said. "You don't have to put up with me."

She crimped her lips and smiled. "I don't think like that."

"Where d'you sleep?"

"In another room."

She rose and the lemon scent rose with her. "You rest now. Sleep, you are still tired. It's very quiet here."

Something struck me. "Do you play any type of musical instrument?" I asked.

"No." She shook her head. "You asked because you want me to play something for you?"

"No. I heard some melody when I woke. Beautiful sound."

"Ah." She canted her head to one side and said nothing as she left the room with the pail.

Moments later, she came back into the room while I was feeling gloomy. She sat down on the edge of the bed and gave me what was in her hand. "Open it," she said, smiling.

It was a pocket watch, round and silvery. The cover was engraved with flowers around the fringe, and in the center there was a bird hovering over two nestlings. I flipped open the hinged cover. A melody rose, clinking into the air. Listening, I felt the weight on my heart lifted. All the time, I gazed at a woman's face that was on the inside of the cover. Her hair was brushed back and clasped with a white flower. She had soft and gentle features in her beauty, though they did not look like each other.

The melody wound down to tiny jingles and ended.

"Who's she?" I said, not wanting to close the cover.

"My mother."

"I couldn't tell. Well, it's a picture."

"She has not changed. She always looks like that."

"Who made it for her?"

"My father. She said he loved her so much he carried it with him all the time. Then he gave it to her because she loved it."

"She wants you to remember her," I said, placing the watch in her hand.

The Moon Festival

It took a month for my recuperation. She would meet me outside the opium den my employer frequented. Sometimes it rained, for it rained often now, just before the Moon Festival, and along the unlit streets her raised lantern would shine on the breathtaking, bright red poinciana flowers. On a dark corner, children were catching fireflies in glass jars, and they waved at anyone who passed by. When we looked back, the dark corner was blinking with glow worms. Then, for two nights, I didn't see her. But on the night of Moon Festival, she showed up unexpectedly as I was coming out of the opium den. My heart jumped. We stopped at a street corner, and I took out a moon cake wrapped in waxed paper. Had she not come, I told her, I would have had to eat it alone. I asked her what the four Chinese characters embossed on the rust-colored, wheat-flour crust said. "Mid-Autumn Moon Cake," she replied. We leaned against a wall between two shops and each ate our share. She said she had always loved this pastry filled with red bean paste and lotus seeds. Up Hemp Street, we passed closed shops with unsold toys still dangling on strings in the display windows: colored paper lanterns printed with flowers and animals. There were children's toys bright in the shops' lanterns, and she smiled while gazing at them. Her face was tranquil. I saw the gentle lines that flowed from her nose to her lips, the arch of her throat, the satiny white of her skin. A procession of unicorn dancers pranced down the street. We stood back in the lee of the shop walls as they went by.

The unicorn head bobbed and weaved in the cadence of the drums, its long body a flowing train of red cloth. The first firecrackers that went off startled her, and she laughed. Trailing the unicorn were children carrying their octagon-shaped lanterns. She pointed and said, "Look, the revolving lanterns." They glowed red and yellow as they passed by, and I could see the silhouettes of eight warriors on horseback go around and around. She asked what made them circle, and I explained to her that the lantern's candle created hot air that propelled the figures. I walked with her into the dark alley to the red door of her place. She blew out the light and hugged me. We stood as one in the dark for a long time, and then she broke off and entered the door without looking back. I stood beneath the dark vault of sky. A feeling came over me as old as the earth, as if I had been here eons before, as air, as dust, or as the scent that clung to her.

The Red Poppy

The evenings we spent together whenever my employer wouldn't need me, we just walked through the city streets, sometimes just wandering until our legs gave out. A few nights later, I went up to the opium den where she worked. She was crossing the street. In her hand was a yellow paper lantern. Nimble feet in thick-soled, black Chinese shoes with curved tips. She held her lantern away from me, and it swung to and fro on a thin bamboo rod. She wasn't dressed all in black.

"You still go out and sell that stuff tonight?" I asked her softly.

"No," she said. "Not tonight."

"Why not tonight?"

"I have to help a monk."

"You help . . . what?" I couldn't hear clearly because of her accent.

"A. Monk," she said it slowly this time.

"A monk? A Buddhist monk? There is no Buddhist pagoda in the Chinese quarter."

"He is not Chinese. And it is not in the Chinese quarter."

"Help him? What kind of help he needs?"

"He has to make books so they . . . stay around."

"Oh. So they won't be extinct."

She tilted her head to look at me.

"They will be gone forever," I said, "if he doesn't do what he's doing."

"Yes."

"How does he make them? How can you help?"

"Do you want to see?"

"Sure," I said.

"Do you want to walk with me to the pagoda?"

"Let's go."

It was drizzling when we took to the road. She folded her umbrella, and we walked under mine. She laced her fingers in mine and held the lantern on her side. Droplets of rain spattered on the lantern and occasionally hit the flame. It sputtered. In the quiet, I told her I missed the clanking of coins in her bag. She didn't laugh.

"What's wrong?" I asked.

"Nothing," she said, cutting her gaze away from me.

"You seem like you're not here."

"I'm here. I'm sorry."

"Tell me what's wrong?"

"Are you afraid for me whenever you don't see me?" She turned her shadowed face toward me.

"Yeah."

"Are you mad?"

"Wish I could be there with you every night. I'm not mad."

"No, you are not. I have never seen you mad."

"But I could be."

She gripped my hand. I could feel her sharp fingernails dig into my palm.

"I'll be going back home in three days," she said finally.

"Why?" I turned sharply to her. "To visit your mother?"

"No," she said, "she's dead."

Then she lowered her head and brought her hand to her mouth. I put my arm around her and, leaning my head against hers, said, "I'm sorry." The glow of her lantern held my attention. "Xiaoli." I met her serene stare. In it an unknown world awaited me.

"Yes?"

"Will you come back?"

"I do not belong here."

All I felt was a hollowness inside myself. What would be waiting for her at home? Home? You cannot call a place a home when there is nothing but emptiness around you.

Around the bend where tangles of vines and shrubbery caught our feet, rain felt harder. Wind blew through cane brakes, sweetening the air with an odor of floral decay. She raised her lantern and pointed it toward the muddy bank. White egrets stepped silently in the wet mud, heads cocked, watching with one eye for fish. Seeing the lantern's light, the birds tipped their heads, regarding us. A night bird called down the embankment, which was pale with withering grass. On a pond, a pagoda was perched atop stone bedding.

I was standing before the pagoda's peculiar structure when she set her lantern on the ground, rolled her pants to her knees, and removed her shoes. She looked back at me.

"Are you just going to stand there?" she said.

I did what she did. We waded into the pond until we were knee-deep in water. Her lantern shone on a network of weathered brown wood beams, sloping sharply, leaning against the black rocks. Out of the pond, we stood under the steep, battered roof dotted with lichens in pale gray.

Inside the pagoda, it was pitch dark. Her lantern's light fell over bins and crates and trailed a conical yellow sphere on the floorboard. The air was damp. Everywhere you turned, the mustiness stung your nostrils. The mildewed air was so thick it was brittle.

"Where's he tonight?" I asked her.

"He went to town," she said. "For a death . . . memorial service?"

"Will he be back tonight?"

"No. He has a remarkable voice when he chants the sutra. People want him."

It struck me as odd. She surely knew the monk wouldn't be here. A wind blew through the door, and the lantern's flame danced wildly. Beyond the entrance the bell turret was a gleaming white. An earsplitting thunderclap shook the floor.

She moved the lantern into the corner where it burned, now yellow, now blue, and she lay inclined on the floor, resting her head on the rim of the wooden crate. The side of her face went dark, only the white of her throat glowed. The flame flickered and died. From the eaves rain fell like a curtain. I picked up the lantern and rose. She pulled me back down.

"Let the fire die," she said.

"Might not be safe. I'm thinking of wild animals."

"Let it die." She paused. "Why don't you lie here."

She held her face upturned, a pale tender oval, and her eyes trailed away when my hand touched the curve of her throat, sloping down in the open-necked shirt. Out in the night a nocturnal bird cried. Broken branches clattered like castanets. The rain let up. In the lull, I heard a crack of thunder. The air smelled of rain and sodden leaves, and the wind was warm and wet coming through the door. The scent of wet leaves was in her hair, damp still, tangled and thick. In the fragrance of her skin clung a woodsmoke scent.

When I lay down by her, her hands came up soft and warm, touching my face. I held still, forgetting myself. Warm, fragrant heat clung to her skin. The curve of her throat sloped into the valley of her shoulder. Wind came sweeping through the door, the air infused with a tinge of wet moss. Her curved back, hollowed to kiss the fingertips. Patches of light on her feverish skin, white worms writhing in the sky. Through the open door, lighting shuddered white.

"You ever wear your hair without a plait?" I asked.

"Yes, but rarely. Why?"

I said that my mother when she was young used to wear hers around her head, and it was so long it hung down her back to her waist, and that the only time she let down her hair was after her bath, when it flowed to the ground like the banyan's aerial roots. She smiled at my description, her teeth white in the dark. She found the twists of her plait and undid them with her fingers and ran them through her hair, letting it spread like black satin, and her whole body was a pale white. She opened her arms and held my face against her chest. Her skin was cool, and her heart thumped against my ear. She asked if I had known any woman before her. Yes, I said, wanting to be pure at heart in her aura. "Tell me about her," she said. I became a storyteller and she a curious listener. She asked if I loved the girl, and I said no and took her hand and pressed it against the side of my face as though to calm a sudden, dark, alien agitation that stirred in my heart. "Do you love me?" she whispered. "Yes, I love you," I said, but the palpitation in my heart beat on. "Do you love me no matter what happens?" she asked. "No matter what happens," I said. "Will you go with me to Lijiang?" "Yes," I said, "I will go wherever you want me to." Then I closed my eyes. I saw a red poppy.

The Children of Icarus

In his sleep, Minh heard a noise at the door.

Lan stood by the night table, looking down at him. Her white nightgown shimmered in the glow of the clock dial. Behind her, the door was open a crack.

He pushed himself up on his elbow. "What keeps you up?"

"I don't know," she said in a whisper, as she sat down on the edge of the bed.

He ran his hands through her hair, brushing it back behind her ears. "I miss you."

She tilted her head, trapping his hand against her shoulder. "How much?"

He opened his arms and pulled her to his chest. She held still. "Everyone's in bed except you," he said. There came a hoot of a barn owl behind her house in the suburb of Maryland.

"I'm glad you came to visit me and my family," she said, her face pressed into his chest. "It was dreadful last week during the trip back from school. At home, my sisters said I looked like a sleepwalker."

She raised her face at him. He bent his head and kissed her on the neck, a spot below her earlobe. She parted her lips with a sigh. After he stopped, she cuddled against him.

"You ever kissed anyone before?" He traced the curves of her brows.

"Why'd you ask?"

"I'm jealous."

She smiled, her eyes gleaming. "I have a story about a

jealous wife. You want to hear?"

"Tell me."

"One day," she said, "the king summoned his favorite mandarin and the mandarin's wife into his palace. He'd heard that the wife was unable to bear children. That meant the end of the mandarin's lineage. He offered help. 'I grant you the right to have a concubine,' the king said to the mandarin. 'Hopefully, you would be blessed with a son.' At the wife's silence, he chided her. 'You seem to be in disagreement with my decree, are you not?' She nodded, again in silence. The king said, 'I give you one chance to redeem yourself. If you abide by my decision, you will be rewarded with the cup of tea on your left; if you oppose it, drink the cup of poison on your right.' The wife kowtowed to him, then picked up the cup of poison and drank it. The king sighed and said to the mandarin, 'Your fate has been decided, and I cannot change it for you. Both cups are tea.'"

Lan raised her hand and rested it on the top of his head. "And I didn't date anyone in school either, so your soul can rest in peace."

"Not even in high school?"

Lan sat up. "I didn't have a boyfriend. The closest I came to dating was with an American pen pal while I was a high school junior."

"How could you date someone through correspondence?"

"Ah." She smiled. "At his request, I sent him my picture, though I'd never received his. All I knew was that he was from Chicago and a high school senior. Then, in one letter he told me he was going to Vietnam after his graduation—his first worldwide tour."

"A rich kid, eh?"

"He'd mentioned that his father was one of the top car dealers in the US." Lan rested her head on his shoulder. "One morning in January, he showed up at my house. He was a redhead, tall as a tree. You know that back home only bar girls hung out with American GIs, and you wouldn't see girls with strict upbringing walk with foreigners, especially American

GIs."

He imagined a face from many redheads he'd seen. None formed in his head.

"My dad happened to be home that week from his military service," she said, "and with his limited English managed to tell my pen pal that his daughter was too young for dating. He let my American friend speak to me in the living room, but Dad sat by me." She pressed his palm against her cheek. "My pen pal came back the next day, asked my dad if we could have some privacy to talk. No, my dad said. He'd become so disturbed by his neighbors' curiosity for two days that he told the young American, 'Vietnamese girls don't date foreigners. That is our value system you must understand.' My pen pal was flabbergasted. He said, 'What did I do wrong? All I want is to get to know her.' A persistent kid, he came back the next day, only to face a marine posted on the front porch."

Minh pressed his lips against her forehead. He waited.

"I know my dad was ashamed to see a Westerner seeking a relationship with his daughter," Lan said, and lifted her head from his shoulder. "My upbringing was so strict—all the way down to how I wore clothes. My mom forbade me to wear tight outfits. Once, she made me change my pants—too tight for my legs—before we went to downtown Saigon. Darling, she said, you don't want boys to look at that crease down there."

"Oh dear." He chuckled, then, "So am I your first love?"

"Yes." She snuggled her face against his collarbone. "Do you want your betrothed to be a virgin?"

His Adam's apple jerked.

"Yes," he said. "I didn't have the guts to admit it in front of your friend."

"Dzu?"

"Him. Do you like him?" The man was an ex-pilot during the Vietnam War—barely five years had gone by since the fall of South Vietnam. Most girls thought fliers were hot. The ex-flier sought them out in the bistro's crowd of students the previous week, just before spring break.

"I like him as a friend," Lan said, holding his gaze. "I've

learned a lot about the differences between the privileged class and the deprived class since I knew Dzu. You and I never saw much of our country except Saigon. He did. He never runs out of stories to tell—war stories, cultural stories, folk tales. He makes me homesick. I realize I'm in a foreign country. I can speak its language, live its habits, think its thoughts, but I'll never be a part of it. That's how much he represents Vietnam, at least for me."

"Be careful. You might be taken in by his act."

"Yes, she nodded. "I know you don't like Dzu. I know he's bitter and crude, and he's a friend of mine. But that's about it."

She smiled as he tried to absorb her frankness.

The three of them had been sitting in a night club, and he forgot what caused the fracas when the subject of a girl's virginity came up. "My wife," Lan's ex-pilot friend said, putting his hand on top of Lan's on the table, "she wasn't as pretty as you, but she was pretty enough for me to fall in love with her and marry her."

Minh tried to ignore Dzu's hand still on top of Lan's hand and said to him, "So, you married her for her good looks?"

Dzu said, deadpan, "Because she was a virgin."

Lan winced, and Minh felt as though the man had just touched her between the legs. Minh looked at Dzu's hand still covering Lan's as words rushed out of his mouth, "Virginity is an obsession among Asian men. You know that?"

Dzu snubbed out the cigarette butt in the ashtray and slowly looked at him and said, "Tell me, if you ever fall in love with a girl, sleep with her, then find out she's not a virgin, would you marry her?"

Quickly Minh nodded, and Dzu said, "You're a liar. You're also a hypocrite. Marry a girl who'd lost her cherry to someone? What do you take me for? An idiot? You know, you're such a privileged kid, you have your head in the clouds most of the time—"

"Privileged?" Minh glared at Dzu. "In what sense? My education? I earned that. Maybe you ended up in the wrong place because you didn't have an education. If you feel sorry for yourself, don't blame those who made things happen for themselves."

"You're no smarter than me. Swap shoes, and you won't walk that far."

"You're such a jealous loser. A loser who takes shots at those who made it."

"How 'bout getting off your butt and help those refugees who get here broke?" Dzu said as he held his smirk.

Minh slammed his glass on the table. "I'm not going to get into a patriotism contest with you. Let me set this straight: Don't confuse your value system with mine; don't malign me before you even know me." He stood up. "Let's go, Lan."

Dzu jabbed his finger at him. "Don't start acting like you own her. You don't order her around—not while I'm involved."

"This is getting out of hand," Lan said. "People are watching us."

Dzu sneered. "He's overreacting, Lan. He cracked up."

"I must go," Lan said, her face hardening at Dzu.

The ruckus they made had other people looking in their direction. They left, moving through a veil of bluish cigarette smoke that drifted across the room. He felt violence simmering in his veins, and in his nose the bar smelled like a wet rag just quenched from burning.

Now recalling the incident, he still smoldered with anger. He'd never asked why, never looked deeper at the root of his resentment, until he heard Lan speak again.

"So, if your betrothed isn't a virgin, you won't marry her?"

"Well—"

"Think about it," she said softly.

He took her hand and pressed her palm on his cheek. "Any other questions?"

"You ever thought about a family for us?"

"Only about you." Then he smiled. "Maybe a baby for us."

"Childbirth scares me."

"You'd rather not go through it?"

"I've seen abnormal babies. Typical Mongoloid. Their mothers lived in the defoliated zones during the war."

"Where did you see these babies?"

"In a Saigon hospital during my senior year in high school. We toured the hospital, and one of the children I saw was a Mongoloid. She had only one cross line in her palms, a prominent forehead. Her left foot had six toes, and both her feet and hands could be bent back in the wrong direction. The nurse said that the child had abnormal tear ducts. When she cried, her tears didn't run out onto her eyes but down into her nose, choking her. She had permanent infection of the eyes. She couldn't walk, couldn't talk, except to say 'Mama.'"

"The Agent Orange caused this?"

"Her mother drank water and ate food from the defoliated area. The mother was normal, didn't take any medication during pregnancy, hadn't even been x-rayed. There were no abnormalities in her family for generations." Then she squeezed his hand. "I'm not afraid of childbirth, the pain of it. I'm more afraid of the abnormal childbirth."

"Let's not talk about it."

She cuddled against him. He looked down into her eyes, those coffee-brown eyes crisscrossed with tiny lights. He lowered his face. He felt her lips parted to receive him. His hand felt hot, as if he had a fever. He kneaded her abdomen in circular motion, then stopped. His fingers slipped in through the front of her gown, fumbling at the buttons. She grabbed his hand.

"Please, don't—" she said, panting.

His hand stopped. His breathing labored in her ear. She cupped the back of his hand and meshed their fingers.

"We must wait." She gulped. "I . . . I want to save it 'til we have a bond between us."

He leaned his face into the mass of her hair. In its thick scent, he felt like he'd just lost a golden key.

She phoned him at four-thirty.

"Minh, I need to talk to you. Dzu just called me—"

"What was it about?"

"He invited me over for a farewell dinner. You know he's leaving for California tomorrow?"

"For good? Did you accept his invitation?"

"Yes. That's why I called."

"You shouldn't go."

"I shouldn't go? Why?"

"He's bad news. That's all I can say."

"Minh, just because you don't like him doesn't make him a bad guy. He's a friend. He's leaving, and this is his last night here."

He felt stuck. What did he want to protect her from? He knew his antipathy for Dzu clouded his judgment.

"Lan, keep away from him. I mean it."

"You make him seem like a criminal."

"So, you're going?"

"Don't control me like that, Minh—we're not even married."

Bitterness filled him. He understood her independent nature. He knew he was opinionated. But that only made him feel more miserable.

Now he cranked down his car window and felt a blast of warm air. He squinted. From Lan's rented room in George-town, he used to watch Rock Creek Parkway curve below P Street Bridge and beyond it, farther north, the Oak Hill Cemetery on the hillside. One block up from P Street Bridge was the Buffalo Bridge. She told him that with binoculars you could make out a row of stone Indian heads anchored to the side of the bridge, each wearing a crownlike headdress, sculpted after the life mask of Chief Kicking Bear. You could even see the four colossal bison in patina green guarding the tips of the bridge. But, of course, you couldn't see—she giggled—what the pranksters sometime did to these animals' gonads with red spray paint.

Gentleness tugged at his heart.

He hung out with some friends in a bar through Happy Hour and then went to the waterfront, where they ate at a seafood restaurant. It was dark after dinner. He wandered around, past the fish market brightly lit with a good crowd who loved oysters and mussels and blue crabs from the Chesapeake Bay. The market was smelly and wet, and people ate steamed shrimp and baked red snapper from their brown bags. From the Gangplank Marina, he stood watching transient boaters on the water. Something had been gnawing at him. And he knew why.

It was near ten o'clock when he got home. At the door of his apartment, he heard the phone ring inside. He strode into the living room and grabbed the phone.

"Hello?"

"Minh . . . ." Lan sobbed.

He heard her as though she was burying her head in his shoulder. He waited, the way one waits out a summer downpour.

"Where've you been?" She had difficulty breathing. "I've been calling and calling, but no one answered."

"I went out with some friends to the Wharf. What's the matter?"

She sobbed and didn't stop, as though a dam had burst.

"Dzu . . . he raped me tonight . . . ."

Her words went like a blade up his gut. He tried to speak, but his jaws were numb. In his ear, she stuttered, "I went to his place . . . . He kept telling me he wouldn't be back . . . . He was pathetic." She wheezed, sucking in her breath. "I was so happy about us that . . . . I told him we'd get engaged this Christmas . . . . He got drunk and nasty, didn't let me leave. Then he . . . he . . . ."

"How could you be so naïve?" he shouted. "I told you he

can't be trusted . . . . Christ!"

"I . . . I know it's my fault . . . ." Her sobbing sounded like hiccups.

"For a girl about to be engaged—you went all the way to his place. Jesus. Did you expect him to behave like a monk—after he tried to come on to you at the bistro? You led him on. Good God!"

"Minh—"

"I asked you not to. Didn't I? What did you say to me? You talked about trust. How—"

"Stop it!" she screamed. "Why do you keep pointing fingers? It happened! You hear me? I can't reverse it. Do you care? For me? Do you?"

He fell silent. Hatred drowned him. Whom did he hate? Dzu? Lan? Suddenly, he heard an ambulance siren over the phone.

"Where are you now?" he asked.

She sniffled. "I'm in a pay phone—around the corner from his place." She sounded so hoarse that he could barely hear her.

"What? I thought you were already home. I thought you had enough sense to—Lan! What got into you?"

"What got into me?" She squealed. "I don't know, Minh. Why do you keep interrogating me? Why didn't you ask me just one thing about my condition? Want to know what I look like right now? A hooker! Want to see what I'm like after he was through with me? I can barely walk. But I ran. I just wished I ran into you. I can't tell you how much . . . how much he hurt me . . . I just can't . . . ."

"Stay there, and I—"

He heard her phone clanging against the wall. He heard car horn's blare, then a click followed by a busy signal.

At eight o'clock the following morning he pulled into the cul-de-sac. He got out and walked up the porch. With only a few hours of sleep, he felt as if he were floating. Across the lawn the shadows had receded, and the grass was bathed in the morning sunlight. Flanking the porch steps were trellises now covered with profuse masses of yellow honeysuckle.

The door opened, and he stood face to face with Lan's mother.

"*Thua bác,*" he said.

"*Chào câu,*" she said.

Her greeting sounded restrained. Her face looked as if she were at a funeral. She stepped back to let him in. As they passed the kitchen, he glanced over and met Lan's sisters, Linh, Trang, and Trinh. They stood at the kitchen counter, grating potatoes and dicing carrots.

"*Thua anh,*" they said in chorus.

Her mother gestured for him to sit down. Slowly he lowered himself onto the couch like an old man. She sat in the stuffed armchair, her back to the kitchen. He looked past her, through the sliding-glass door. There the morning sky was brightening, and here in the house the quiet made him soften his voice.

"How is she?"

"She's coming around. But she was a wreck last night." Lan's mother's voice wavered. "I made her scrub herself till her skin chafed—then she did what needs to be done for precaution."

"I told her not to go to his place. I told her to watch out for him."

"She's very trustful. That sometimes can be a curse, too."

He thought how the law would find the rapist if her family hadn't reported the rape. But then he realized that most Asian families would rather protect their names than seeing their daughter's name dishonored in public.

"Where is she now?"

"In the park." Lan's mother squared her shoulders. "She wants to be alone."

"But I need to see her."

"Why not last night when she needed you most?" She

stared at him, head tilted. "Didn't she call you after it happened?"

The edge in her voice, the look in her eyes made him want to hide. He lowered his gaze and stared blindly at his knees.

"I was angry with her and let it get the better of me." He looked up at Lan's mother. "I thought about it and am here to ask her to forgive me. I hope you understand."

"I'm sure you weren't the victim of circumstances like her. It was very hard for me—and for her—to accept your act."

"I'm sorry."

She motioned with her sweeping finger. "Once you have the matrimonial thought already in your head, you should leave your little self behind." She rose. "You know how to get to the park in the back of our house, don't you?"

The word *yes* was stuck in his throat as he brought himself to his feet. She paced ahead of him, and, following her, he saw Lan's sisters wave at him like characters in a silent movie. She kept the door open until he got out, then shut it behind him.

He walked around the house and into the woods behind it, following a bike trail that cut through the park. Glancing back, he saw their garden hemmed in by the white fence. Then the trees blocked his view.

He rounded the curve and heard the rushing sound of a brook. The bank sloped down to the water coursing over boulders. The water looked dark under the trees, their branches laced into a long arch. The empty trail skirted the brook and, upstream, opened out into a field. He stopped when he saw Lan sitting on a bench by herself.

In the distance, she looked small, a figure in a gray sweatshirt. She wore a straw hat. He watched her the way a traveler coming home might watch the smoke rise from the chimney of his house.

Slowly, he walked up to her. His eyes never left her as he saw only a part of her face, the rest covered by her wide-brimmed straw hat. She sat with her back straight, knees pressed together, and hands laced in her lap. Her posture reminded him of a pose for a portrait.

When he was near, she looked up. The shock in her eyes made him stop short.

"Lan—"

He sat down by her. He could hear her sharp intake of breath as he bent forward to seek her eyes. He saw the reddish marks on her jawline, on her throat. His heart contracted with a violent tug. Those marks left by the beastly rape could have passed for skin rash.

"I need to speak for myself—" He dropped his voice, "—despite what happened."

She turned to face him, the brim of her hat brushing his brow. Her eyes were puffy.

"Tell me what you have to say." Her voice was still hoarse.

"I lost my mind when I heard what he did to you." His hand found hers, then froze as she withdrew it.

"I was going to call you later," she said, "and ask you to forget about our relationship."

"I'm here because I love you," he said. "Will you forgive me?"

He put his hand on the back of hers. This time she let him. "Last night," he said, "must be the longest night ever for you."

She said nothing.

"Did you sleep?" he asked. "Or did you not?"

"Linh slept with me. I guess she probably didn't have much sleep, either, because of my crying."

He took a sharp breath.

"I wish I never met him," she said, crimping her lips. "Never knew him. He turned on me—just like that."

He dropped his gaze to the ground. His head was full of murderous thoughts.

"Every time I closed my eyes, I saw him . . . ." She took off her hat and held it in her lap. "Then that scene came back . . . ."

He put his arms around her, and she rested her head on his shoulder. He could smell staleness in her hair.

"I went crazy with his smell on my body when I got back,"

she said. "His disgusting cologne on my hands, on my arms, everywhere. His sweat . . . smelled like ammonia, and it stayed on my skin. I prayed that . . . you were here with me last night."

Her body felt stiff. He closed his eyes, saw himself trapped with his evil thoughts.

"Lan." He pressed his lips on the top of her head. "I want to ask you if—"

"If I get pregnant?"

That felt like an electrical shock. *Damn.*

"What will you do?" he asked.

She fell into a long silence. He thought she didn't breathe. Then she said, "I thought about that. I had a long talk with Mom last night. She . . . ."

"What did she say?"

"She didn't want to see me go through it."

"And how do you feel about it?"

"I'm against killing life—any life."

He gripped the slats of the bench to brace himself. It would be much easier if she accepted her mother's opinion. It would be much easier for everyone. But if he could put himself in her place, be a victim, be her body . . . if he could only stop thinking about himself . . . .

"Will you go through this with me if it happens?" she asked.

He sucked in his breath. The notion was revolting.

"Damn," he said, loud.

Immediately, she jerked her head back. "What?"

"Please let me explain."

She shook her head, grimacing.

"I wish I could go back in time and undo it," he said, stroking her on the back between her shoulder blades as if to ease her shaking. "Just like you wish you never met Dzu. The whole thing's sickening."

"Stop. Please stop."

"If you want me to."

"Stop it!"

She turned her body away. His hands slipped down from her back, and again he gripped the slats of the bench. She shivered. Her nose dripped, and she let it. The ground sucked his feet into it. He spoke to her back.

"I love you," he said. "And I don't care what will happen."

"Please don't say it for the sake of saying."

"Sorry, I can't just shrug it off."

"If you love me, then help me accept and love what God intends for us. Bad things, too."

"I understand. But it's so sudden—before I knew it."

She leaned her forehead against his. He could hear her choke on her inhalation. Then, in a scratchy voice she said, "I love you."

He held her, like holding a mannequin. Her spasms went through to his fingertips. She lifted her face to him. Along her jawline were red marks. He laced his fingers behind the back of her neck and kept his voice level. "I'm sorry. I cared only about my loss and forgot yours."

Her eyes softened. He cupped her face and kissed her on the forehead.

"Can we go back in?" he asked.

Slowly, they rose and headed for the house. Beneath their feet, the leaves crackled as they walked down the trail. His head bent forward; he watched their shadows moving in front of them on a slant. Her body felt limp in his arm. He slowed down, and their feet caught.

"Let's sit," he said. "You're out of breath."

They knelt by the edge of the brook in the shade. On the wet grass a mantis rose, clasping a grass blade with its forelimbs. He could see the brook's bottom where massive white and tan boulders overlapped, dotted with bluish and gray pebbles.

She placed her hat over the mantis. "Will you be honest with me?" she said.

"What bothers you?"

"You were the one who said you would marry a girl who's no longer a virgin."

"I lied to Dzu." Then he pressed her hands against his heart. "I love you—with everything here."

Nodding, she closed her eyes.

He dipped his hands in the water. Bluegills darted with quick shadows. The water felt cool. He dabbed water on her face, and she shut her eyes. Then he bent and pressed his face into his cupped hands.

He opened his eyes and saw in the water Lan's face looking up at him. For the first time, she smiled.

All the Rivers
Flow into the Sea

The American followed Phuong onto a wide-bottomed boat. It went downriver in the shadow of kapok trees glowing red with tiny blossoms. The afternoon sun glared on her face. With his handkerchief, the American dabbed her perspiring cheeks, and she bit her lower lip, holding her face still. People looked at them.

They talked in low voices, putting their heads together so they could hear. The American sat with his hands between his knees, smiling at strange faces. The boat kept close to the bank. The wind spun the petals of kapok blossoms against the reddening sky.

When she woke, her hand was in his, and the boat touched the bank. Phuong asked around. They would have to continue on foot until they found another boat going south. The train bound for Hue had turned back, because somewhere south the Viet Cong had seized a town, and the South Vietnamese army was coming to take it back.

Phuong stood among a small gathering of men and women on the red earth that changed to yellow beyond glistening sand dunes. Next to her, the American surveyed the landscape.

"Are you sure you want to do this, Phuong?" he said to her in heavily accented Vietnamese.

"I'm more than sure, Jonathan." She shielded her eyes. "I'm worried only about you."

"Me?"

"Can you make it?"

The American nodded firmly.

Ahead of them walked a woman carrying a little girl in one arm. With her other hand, she clutched a cloth bag and pulled a small boy along. The little girl in the woman's arms moaned about thirst. As hawks called overhead, they crossed a woodland thick with the smell of fallen pine needles, soft as brown velour. The little girl cried, "Snake!" pointing to a brown woody vine creeping around a eucalyptus tree.

From deep in the woodland came the sound of water, a stream as clear and shallow as it was cold. They drank from their cupped hands. The American splashed water on his face, letting it run down the front of his shirt. Next to him, the woman washed her children with a handkerchief. The boy said he was hungry.

The silvery railroad track flashed in the distance. Sweat dripped down Jonathan's face, and the sun's glare on the conical hats had him shade his eyes with his hand. He asked Phuong if she wanted to rest. She wet her lips.

"We must press on. Do you want to rest, Jonathan?"

"Don't worry about me," he said.

Soon the little boy fell behind, hobbling in pain. His mother held his torn rubber thongs and pulled him along. He tried to walk on the ties and cried when the sharp gravel cut his feet. The woman wrapped them with a sleeve she tore from a shirt. Jonathan looked back. The boy was limping along behind his mother, who carried the little girl on her hip.

Phuong tugged Jonathan's arm. "Can you carry him?"

"Of course."

The mother thanked him profusely when he let the boy climb onto his back. Jonathan smiled at the little girl, who smiled back and yawned. He walked beside Phuong, the mother trailing behind.

Then the little girl asked, "Mom, can Mr. American see like us? His eyes are blue. How do you make them blue?"

The boy cut in. "You don't. They're just blue."

The girl giggled. "His hair, Mommy, it looks like duck down."

Phuong smiled. "Why don't you ask him something?"

"What's your name, Mister?" the girl said in Vietnamese.

Jonathan turned to look at her. "Jonathan. And what's yours?"

The girl hid her face on her mother's shoulder. The woman looked embarrassed and smiled nervously. "Tell Mr. Jonathan your name."

"My name is Châu."

Jonathan patted the boy's leg. "And what's your name?"

"Cung."

"Good. Are you afraid, Cung?"

"No. Mommy said it's scary only if you have to walk through the jungle."

"Why?"

"Because the orangutans will get you. Mommy said if you have to walk through the jungle, you put your arms in two bamboo tubes."

"Why?"

"Because when they grab you, they grab your arms, so you slip them out of the bamboo tubes and run for your life."

Jonathan laughed. "Is that for real?"

"It's for real, Mr. Jon-a-than," Cung said.

The little girl piped up. "If you go through the jungle, you have to bring an old bicycle tire tube and cut it up into rubber bands."

"Why can't you just bring rubber bands? Why do you need rubber bands in the jungle?"

"They don't sell them around here. Only in the city. And you need them because the jungle leeches come down from the trees after a rain. They get into your pants and suck your blood."

"I'm glad we're not going through the jungle."

"If we do," Cung said, "you think the orangutans would be scared?"

"Why?"

"There are a lot of us. And the orangutans are smaller than you."

"Thanks, Cung. I feel important now."

Phuong looked back at Jonathan. His face was sweaty and red from the sun, and he walked stooped, the boy draped on his back, his skinny arms locked around Jonathan's neck. She stopped and waited for him. He smiled. She forgot her own thirst when she saw his lips dry from dehydration.

Late afternoon, they came to a hut where an old woman sold refreshments. Gone quickly were a few bundles of bananas, then rice waffles. Phuong asked the old woman if she had something else for the children, and the woman began to grate cassava. She sprinkled brown sugar on shredded white cassava, wrapped a good portion of it in a green banana leaf. Before she tied it up, she slit the middle of the cassava mound and filled it with mung bean. She filled a rack with cassava rolls and lowered it into a boiling crock. The children sniffed the fragrant steam. She gave each a chipped clay plate and dropped on it a steaming cassava roll. They blew and ate with their fingers and wanted more before they cleaned their plates. Their mother said she had to save money for boat fare, and their dejected faces moved Jonathan to buy them. While Phuong talked to people outside, he watched the children eat.

The woman owner said they could wait until night to catch a boat, then dropped her voice and warned them that they were in a war zone controlled by Mr. Viet Cong.

At night the river was black, and the bank gleamed with the ivory-colored conical hats. People held onto one another on the clay slope, waiting. Boats came and went. Hushed. They said each boat traveled downriver in blackness, in silence, to slip through the Viet Cong checkpoint. The crowd got smaller. In the quiet came the sound of the river lapping the bank.

Phuong and the mother said they'd go together, so when a boat had room only for two more passengers, they decided to wait for the next one. It came much later, carrying bundles of bananas piled to the rim of its rattan shelter. The boatwoman said she would take them to the next village. Phuong asked her about the town the Viet Cong had captured and was told they would bypass it on the river, but the fighting was fierce.

Late at night the river became busy with boats going up- and downriver without lights. Sitting on the floor, the American leaned against the wall of green bananas. Starlight fell on the river, bobbing like silver sequins. He sat with his knees against his chin, while the children lay across their mother's thighs, looking up at the stars, at the yellow and green specks of fireflies blinking in the bushes.

Phuong stretched her legs, looking at her white ankles in the moonlight. She could see black lines on her chapped heels, clad in black rubber sandals. She rested her head on Jonathan's shoulder, her eyes shut, breathing quietly. She thought of her father. The morning before she left with Jonathan, a neighbor came to drink tea with her father, who was blind in both eyes from cataracts. While she was gone, the neighbor would look after him. He still had recurring stomach pain and nausea but said he would be fine, that it would soon pass. She brought him a hot water bottle, and he slept with it. If she had the money, she would take him to the best doctor in Hue. The day before she left, she gave Mrs. Xinh, a well-known trader in Gia-Linh, two hundred thousand đồng—most of her savings—investment money she could not get to for the next three months. It had to pay off.

Jonathan pressed his cheek against the top of her head, touching her braid with his fingers. He had met her in her noodle shop in Gia-Linh near Hue. It was a small noodle shop, where twelve customers sat around six small wooden tables, and a rich, spicy smell always hung in the air. He told her, in Vietnamese, that he was with the Agency for International Development. At sunset he would show up at her noodle shop and walk her home. She walked fast, shouldering two oversize copper pots bobbing on a shoulder pole. Though out of breath trying to keep up with her, the American offered to help, and she told him she was used to the weight, that she left home at six-thirty every morning with two fully loaded pots. He asked how she could shoulder such a load back and forth every day. He didn't know that nothing is hard once it becomes routine.

The first time he asked her how far she lived from the market, she said it was about four kilometers, and the cross-village bus seldom ran her route. The road would curve around a field, a world of green sugarcane leaves. The cane field was so still in the late summer afternoon heat you could hear the rustle of leaves beneath the lull of cicadas.

The first time they had met, she wore a scarlet blouse. He said her bright red blouse gave him pause. She asked what else. He told her that she was the girl he built his dreams on, and she laughed at the way he praised her. It sounded awkward and funny to hear him speak the words in Vietnamese. When she had to travel to Quang Tri to see her dying uncle, Jonathan told her that it was a war zone and convinced her to let him accompany her. Before they left, he bought her father a gift—some rare tea in a golden canister. At the train station, he followed her, pushing, elbowing through crowds of people who never formed lines or apologized for being rude. He shielded her to get her safely up the steps to the coach. Once he went to the latrine, stepping over bodies curled up on the floor. When he came back, he complained that he couldn't stand upright in the latrine. It wasn't built for Westerners. From their bench Phuong looked at the people climbing onto the train. Women in torn, unbuttoned blouses nursed babies. Swollen nipples filmed white. Children cried. Watching them, she believed it must dawn on the American in such a moment that the pacification program training had never taught him what poverty was like, how tenuous life was in the grip of war and shortage of food.

Now she could smell the river, and its muddy odor stirred her pity for the barren earth, its poverty, its people struggling for mere subsistence.

An upriver boat passed them in the dark. The boatman, leaning over the gunwale, barked out words, all muffled. The boatwoman signaled for Phuong to come to the stern. When she came back, Phuong told them that the Viet Cong was setting up a checkpoint farther downriver. She said the boatwoman believed they'd take the American prisoner if they saw him.

"We can't drop you off here," Phuong said to Jonathan. "This is Viet Cong country."

"How about if I hide?" Jonathan said.

"Where? We have to pass through the checkpoint. We can't stop here. It's not even safe in daytime."

He pointed at the wall of bananas. "I'll hide under there."

"What?" the mother said.

"There's no other choice. Do it quick," Phuong said, then cupped her hand and whispered a message to the boatwoman.

They hurried to move bananas to the bow. Phuong told the mother to wake her children. "Tell them what we're doing. He doesn't exist if the Viet Cong ask them."

Jonathan lay on his side on the wet deck of the boat. The children squatted and touched his feet.

"Don't be scared, Mr. Jon-a-than," Cung said.

The American raised his hand to thank the boy but quickly brought it back down as they piled bundles of bananas on top of him. The smell of the old tar that coated the floor, the stink of betel and tobacco spit, hung about him. Soon there was only the cadence of the oar.

The boat slid to a stop. A man flashed a light on the bank. Voices.

"How many people?"

"Three women, two children," the boatwoman said.

"You carry rice?"

"No, Sir, just bananas."

The boat rocked as the man stepped onto it. His voice rose. "You don't carry rice under these bananas?"

"No, Sir, I don't sell rice."

The man grunted. "You people are sneaky."

Nobody said anything. The flashlight wavered. The man filled a bucket with water and splashed it against the mound of bananas. Water dripped, collecting on the deck. The man splashed three more buckets of water. *Please stop*, Phuong pled in her head. Water was sluicing between her feet.

"How many bundles of bananas?" the man asked.

"I don't know, Sir," the boat woman said. "I didn't count."

Phuong froze when she saw the man flash his lamp over an opening in the heap of bananas. The light moved from one opening to another. Then he dropped the bucket onto the deck of the boat. His voice shot out, "Tax: two hundred đồng."

Soon the boat moved back out. A short distance downriver, they began clearing the pile of bananas. The American pushed himself up, dripping wet.

"Jonathan!" Phuong said, grabbing his arm.

The boy shook her arm. "I told you, Auntie, he'll be okay."

Still shaken, the American sat down, looking shrunken and insignificant.

She asked her father after they had arrived home to let Jonathan stay the night, because it was too late for him to go back to town. A foreign correspondent was killed a few months before in Gia-Linh. Her father said the Viet Cong buried him alive in the sugarcane field. They believed he was CIA.

She cooked gobies simmered with fragrant knotweed, pumpkin soup with prawns and fresh garden vegetables— thin slices of tomato around the platter's edge above yellow star-shaped carambola and half-moon strips of purple figs in the center. They sat barefoot on the mahogany divan under a dome-shaped lamp. In the soft yellow light, the American watched them, then crossed his legs, struggling to rest a foot on the opposite thigh. The gobies were hot. His eyes watered from the black peppercorns cooked with the fish. She ate slowly, waiting for him. She corrected the way he held the chopsticks. "Like this," she said, making him grip them higher.

After he washed in the bathhouse in the rear, Jonathan came back to the mahogany divan to sleep. Next to a white pillow lay a neatly folded woolen blanket. He had turned down her offer to let him use her bed for the night and said he would sleep on the divan without a mosquito net.

A kerosene lamp burned dimly on a table in a corner. Her

body aching, Phuong lay under the blanket, eyes open, looking up at the ceiling. Behind the curtain in a corner, her father snored. A dog barked in the distance, then another. A whine by her ear. She slapped the invisible mosquito, then pulled the blanket over her head.

She didn't know the time when she slid down from her cot, quietly unlatched the door, and walked out into the garden. The milky light of a full moon glowed in every corner, and the night wasn't black but blue, bluer than indigo. The trees lay a smooth shade around the house. Cobblestones crunched underfoot. Moss grew on the stucco walls, the green discolored with the years.

She walked along the edge of the garden, where bamboo and screw pines grew thick and the nightshade let no light through. Walking so close to them, she heard the squeaking of bamboo trunks, the murmur of leaves. From inside the house came a groan, clear in the stillness.

In the rock basin, the water seemed blacker than ever beneath the canopy of the milk apple. A paper lantern hung on a limb of the grapefruit tree. A frail scent of grapefruit blossoms as she passed under. The night lit like a yellow shawl made of something so filmy that a touch would make it disappear. In the stillness she felt transparent. No bone, no flesh, no identity. Light shone through, scents of fragrant pines, of the brown earth, acrid and old.

She walked back to the courtyard and saw Jonathan standing by the rock island under the dark parasol of the milk apple. His shirt was the only white.

"Your father," he said to her, "had some pain again tonight."

She looked at him. "I thought you'd be sound asleep tonight."

"The mosquitoes kept me awake."

"Really? I thought it was my father's moaning."

He laughed softly. "That too."

"I gave him a hot water bottle to calm it."

"Phuong, he must see a doctor tomorrow. I'll go with you."

"You don't have to."

"That's in Hue, isn't it?"

"Yes. A long way. When are you going back to America?"

"In a few days, but I can delay it." A scent trailed in the air. He breathed in deeply. "Where's that scent coming from?"

She pointed toward a thicket of shrubs in a corner. "The Chinese call it *Yeh-lai-hsiang*, night fragrance."

"Such a lovely scent."

She brushed her hair with her fingers. "Will you come back?"

"I don't want to leave at all."

She thought for a moment. Perhaps in love there's no coming or going.

Early in the morning she took her father to a free clinic in Hue. In the ocher-colored waiting room, she could smell a musty odor. Late the night before, when Phuong had emptied his chamber pot because he was too weak to go to the outhouse, she found a trace of blood in his stool. At his age, he took one day at a time. Death didn't frighten him, he had told her, but the prospect of heavy medical costs did.

Phuong opened her eyes. The doctor and a nurse were walking her father out after a long examination. She rose just as the nurse helped her father sit down.

"Your father has colon cancer," the doctor said. "All the tests came out positive. He has large lesions in several places in his colon. I strongly recommend radiotherapy as soon as possible. We need to see him once a week until we see improvement."

"How much does the treatment cost?"

"Our office can tell you."

She thanked him and told her father she'd be back. She paid for the examination and got the estimate for the radiotherapy. Six months of treatment: 110,000 đồng. When she came back to her father, she felt light-headed. She took his hand and walked him out of the hospital into the sunlight. They waited on the curb for the pedicab. She grew dizzy in the bright sun.

The American had borrowed a bike, and he took Phuong to Mrs. Xinh's. In the afternoon sun they rode past a roadside shrine. Phuong asked him to stop, went in, and lit joss sticks in the dark room. *May your power sustain Father through his illness*, she whispered a prayer to the road deity, then bowed deeply to the porcelain statue of a bearded man whose bulging eyes and black beard conveyed a ferocious mien.

When they rode on, Jonathan asked her, "What's the shrine for?"

"For wayfarers on this road."

"I see them everywhere."

"My father can tell you more about the magical powers we believe in. That's why we have a shrine for the road, a shrine for the rice paddy, a shrine for the river. But the gods will help you only if you're desperate for the welfare of others, not for yourself."

They biked under the cool shade of giant trees. "What are those trees, Phuong?" he asked her.

"*Bàng*. We use their nuts to stuff cakes because almonds are expensive. In autumn their leaves are very red. What's the name of the Dutch artist who painted his self-portrait with an ear missing?"

"Van Gogh?"

"Yes, like the reds he used."

"And those trees with tiny white flowers like Japanese apricot flowers?"

"*Mù u*. Children use the seeds to shoot marbles."

Jonathan laughed. "Did you shoot marbles when you were a kid?"

"Yes, Father taught me. But that was years ago."

She fought back tears after they left Xinh's house. She held it in while Jonathan pedaled in silence until they came upon the shrine. Then her sobs stopped him. He got off the bike.

"What happened, Phuong?"

She cupped her face in her hands and sobbed. He held her against his chest.

"I lost my investment," she said.

"What investment?"

She told him about Xinh and the cargo boat she put her money into. She told him it sank coming back from Hôi An, so all was lost.

The American shook his head. "You do business on a handshake?"

Phuong stared at him, her eyes wet.

"Do you have a receipt showing how much you gave her?"

"Sure, I do. But what good is it after what she told me? She took a loss, too."

"How do you know it's true? You're too trusting."

She sobbed again, her body shaking. She was counting on getting the money back for her father's treatment.

"You have nothing left?"

"Enough to keep the business going and our daily expenses. But that's all." She bit her lower lip hard. "Can you take me home? It's getting dark, and you need to get back, too."

They rode on. She thought of the shrine and wondered if the road deity turned a deaf ear to her. At her house, Phuong got off the bike, and Jonathan turned and took her hand.

"Phuong."

She looked at him. He looked tired, his blue eyes dark. He took off his navy-blue worker cap and pushed the hair off his forehead.

"Can I ask you something?" he said.

"Ask me anything."

"Will you let me help you pay your father's medical

expenses?"

Words of gratitude rose to her lips, but she did not speak.

"Does that mean yes?" he asked.

She shook her head and said, "Let me talk to Father. He's so proud. He may not feel comfortable taking anything from you."

"Tell him his health is important to me, just like your happiness. I can help. Let me."

"You can eat with us," she said, forcing a smile.

Her father took only a few slurps of vegetable soup, complaining that he had no appetite. He asked for a piece of brown sugar to get rid of the flat taste on his tongue. She gave it to him and was struck by the strength of his teeth as he cracked it. All of them still there, lacquered black and retouched over the years. When he asked for his tea, she poured him a cup and told him about the loss of her investment. He listened, rolling the chip of brown sugar in his mouth.

"How much?"

She told him.

He stopped chewing. "Was that all you had?"

"More or less."

"What kind of woman is she?"

"She knows business, knows lots of people. She has money."

"But your whole savings?" He clucked. "You'd better find out where and how her boat sank—and how much cargo was on it."

She recalled Jonathan's doubt. Could it be a sham? She felt the thickness in her throat again. She did not want to believe someone would do that to her.

"That won't get back my money, Father."

"Can you think of a better way?"

She told him of Jonathan's offer to help, and her father considered what she said.

"In my whole life," he said finally, "I have never begged or stooped to take a handout from anyone."

"Jonathan does not see it as a handout, Father. I'm sure of that."

"Sir," Jonathan said.

The old man's blind eyes peered blankly into space.

"Sir," Jonathan said again, "Will you let me help pay for the cancer treatment?"

"Have you ever seen anybody cured of cancer?" The old man's wrinkled face was lined with the imprint of the rush mat.

"I don't know, Sir. I'm too young to know much."

"They can treat you so you don't die right away, but you will still die, only slowly."

"But there's a chance that you'd live."

"That's an illusion."

"Maybe that's your way of thinking."

"And what is your way?"

"Sir," Jonathan said, hunching forward on the divan, "I want her to be happy, and the way is for you to get well again."

The old man said nothing. Outside it was dark. The American looked uneasy, as if he must take leave or chance riding home on unsafe roads at night.

"Will you let her accept my money? Will you accept it, Sir?"

The old man peered into a space before him, then he searched for Jonathan's hand, found it, and patted it. "You're very kind. Your offer will be on my mind."

"I hope time will bring you real happiness, Sir. I can say I've found happiness with your family."

The old man scratched the side of his face with a curving fingernail. "Each day I open a door and walk through a corridor of that day and feel thankful if I make it to the end. Every day since Phuong was a teenager. I've opened thousands of doors, and I've always come back to the first one. Because I was afraid that I'd die before she grew up. Now she's an adult, and there are a few doors left unopened for me.

I know one has no corridor." Then he smiled peacefully. "But I have no fear of death—it's inevitable—only the fear of leaving her uncared for."

Phuong stopped eating. A well of gratitude opened up in her. She sat, head down, gazing at her lap. Her father put his bowl and chopsticks down and said to the American, "You have my deepest gratitude for your good heart."

Jonathan smiled. "Thank you, Sir. I'll be back tomorrow with the money."

The next day Phuong waited at her noodle shop until dark, but the American didn't come. The sun seemed stationary, its glare steady on the front of the shop. The day stood still, and it was busy. The south wind blew dust in, and she had to let the rush mat down over the entrance to keep it out. She took a chunk of beef from an icebox and started slicing. Pink slices, lean, veined white with tendons.

Later she sliced more beef and watched customers come in and startled each time the rush mat was pushed aside. She cut her finger and dripped blood onto the beef. She stuck the end of her finger in a lemon wedge. When the blood stopped, she put on a cotton ball and tied it down. It smarted when she crooked her finger, and she told herself not to hurry. Still, she started dropping things as the day waned and the sunlight darkened to bronze on the rush mat.

She put away all the utensils, wrapped up the beef tenderized in pineapple, and covered it with ice. He must have forgotten. No, she thought, impossible. Perhaps he was sick.

She headed home, her two empty pots swinging on her shoulder pole, the lantern in her hand shining about her feet. She watched the lantern because its leaf-shaped flame harnessed her mind. As she watched the lantern, Jonathan came into her vision, tiny as the quivering flame in suffused yellow. A sudden gust of wind blew the lantern out. She tried to light it in the strong breeze, but the match went out.

Phuong sat down on the shoulder, her back to the wind, struck a match, and held it against the wick. The flame wavered and then shone steadily. She lowered the lantern over a dark red pool running off the edge of the road onto the ochre-colored dirt.

The damp dirt glistened in the lantern light, and the dark stain trailed into the field. She saw the dusky color of blood. Her heart suddenly went gray.

She stayed on the ground, staring into the dark cane field. Then she shouted, "Jonathan!" and heard the wind blow her voice away.

When she got home, she asked her father if Jonathan had come by.

"Yes," her father said. "He brought the money they wired him. He said he'd head for your shop. Did he, Phuong?"

"He never came. Do you know where he might've gone to?"

She told her father what she saw on the road. He rose from his stool, groping with his feet for his sandals. "Take me there."

Their neighbor and his son went with them to the cane field. The bloodstains had dried in the dirt. The search party stood on the edge of the road, swinging their lanterns in front of them and peering into the dark field.

Phuong and the men left her father on the road and went single file into the field. A night bird shot up among the stalks, its cry startling them. She looked to the ground and saw the American, facedown, his navy-blue worker cap askew on his head. The side of his neck was slashed.

Her vision clouded, the lanterns seemed to sway. She felt chilled, the cold coming not from the air but from within her. When she couldn't make out Jonathan's face anymore, she realized she was crying, and, regaining her senses, she rose to her feet.

"Can you please carry him out?" she said to two men.

❖

Dawn.

Pale light fell on her father's eyes, so familiar he once said to her he could foresee the weather. She held open the mosquito net and let him ease himself out of the cot. He walked barefoot to the divan and sat down. He struck a match. Before his eyes a sphere lit up. It was like something bright behind a translucent screen. He ran his palm over the brazier's coals, as he always did, and a faint heat told him the coals were catching flame.

He had slept well during the night, his body benign save an occasional abdominal pain from the cancer treatment that started a month earlier. Every Monday. Like clockwork. He told her it would be a warm Monday, when he dressed for the treatment trip to Hue.

As the coals popped, she sat down on the divan with a tray. The smell of hot gruel warmed the air.

"I bought some sweets for you yesterday, Father."

He took a finger-long candy wrapped in cellophane paper and unwrapped it. It was a chewy caramel coated with sesame seeds.

She took the candy from his hand. "You go on and eat your porridge. I'm going to make tea, and then you can enjoy the candy."

"Get me the tribute tea, Phuong. I have a craving for it with caramel candy."

He picked up the thick, glazed bowl. A small slab of brown sugar floated in it. He stirred the gruel with the ceramic spoon, round and round, until the brown sugar shrank, marbling the white gruel. Then, he lifted the spoon and sipped. At the credenza where he kept tea and the tea set, she stood holding the golden canister. Neither her father nor she had touched it since Jonathan had given it to him. She looked at it and cried.

More than a month now since they sent his body back home. Her father and she prayed for him often. He prayed when she wasn't home. One night, waking from sleep as she often did, she listened for his moans. Pain was habit. It roused you from sleep at a certain time in the night, and your body remembered it like a timetable. All was quiet. Relieved, she lay awake.

She recalled the night Jonathan had spent with them. Sweet memory. If a stretch of river was haunted, people built a shrine to pacify the spirits. Perhaps someday they should build a shrine by the cane field. By the constant praying, the lost souls of the dead would find eternal peace. Maybe Jonathan would come home again in his own ethereal world. Her father believed his soul wasn't trapped in the world of darkness. A good soul. All goodness.

That night she cried and heard her father stir and knew he was awake hearing her. Her crying kept him awake a long time, but he didn't comfort her. Solitude had its own moments. Bitter and sweet. It would eventually die into itself.

After her father drank a third cup of tea, the fire was dim but warm. Outside on the doorstep she took his hand and stood beside him. Three steps went down, and he still let her walk him after all the years.

"Father," she said softly.

"What is it?"

"Our flame tree is covered in red."

Then the cicadas began to sing.